For Jen,
May your
mostly

KEEN

May any
sorrow
be worth
the
love
it
brought
you.

And with best wishes
for your own writing!

Erin Stalcup
Oct. 20 '21

ISBN 978-1-7377808-0-9
Copyright © Erin Stalcup, 2022
Published by Gold Wake Press
Cover design by Marielena Andre
Book interior by Paul Brooke
Keen 2022, Erin Stalcup
goldwake.com

"The ugly fact is books are made out of books, the novel depends for its life on the novels that have been written."

—Cormac McCarthy

Nah.
This book is dedicated to my entire lineage.
Thank you.

PART ONE
CHAPTER ONE

Paparazzi bulbs burst on Maeve's skin like heat lightning. We were always surprised they didn't leave a mark—she was so pale, and they were more incandescent than the sun. She posed next to Hungry, her date, who was so covered in fabric and makeup we knew she couldn't feel the flashes. Hungry didn't smile because it would ruin the effect of her face, her misshapen mouth, her drawn-on cheekbones and black eyes. Maeve McNamara, the most famous keener in the world, didn't smile because it would ruin her reputation. We loved their look for this awards show, Hungry in all white, which didn't make her any less frighteningly uncanny, face mask of jaws ending in pinchers and jewels, lips more like an orchid than an orifice, her teeth-mountain chest tattoo the only skin exposed, long gloves and a corseted wide-legged pantsuit, high heels. Maeve was in a black de la Renta lace sheath, v-neck and low-backed, to let her gleaming skin show. Her dark hair was up in a simple bun, only azalea-pink gloss and long lashes, her star chart of freckles not hidden. She was wearing strings of bright diamonds in her ears, rows of diamond sparks on her fingers—we loved watching her borrowing things—and nude Manolo Blahniks she didn't have to give back. We enjoyed her slim silhouette against Hungry's voluminous charisma, the austere next to the ostentatious, and we hoped we'd finally get to see them kiss tonight.

At some point, we just admitted we didn't know how to mourn. We, the de-ethnicized people in the United States. Jewish people know how to mourn.

Catholic people know how to mourn. Mexican people know how to mourn. Indigenous people know how to mourn, within their individual tribal customs. But some of us have been here so long we forgot where we were from. Some of us were taken here, made to forget where we were from.

A cultural framework shows us what to do, makes some decisions so we're less at sea for how to process this thing that is impossible to process. *They are gone.* So. Wear black. Wear white. Sit shiva for seven days, forget about comfort, cover the mirrors, forget about appearance, that doesn't matter now. Then stand up and go back to your life. Walk in jazz funeral processions, and the music will move from dirges to dance tunes. Chop up the body, and feed it to the vultures. Bury the dead in a coffin shaped like something they loved in life, a rose or race car or guitar. A year after their death, disinter the body and dance with it, dress it in new clothes, throw a parade, tell them all the news. Dismember, roast, and eat the dead. Kill a member of another tribe to satisfy your rage. Throw a shovelful of dirt on the coffin, each mourner. Take pictures of the embalmed body. Keep locks of hair. Leave the body with useful tools, your best jewelry, flowers, prepare them for the other side. Communities around the world still know what to do. But some of us lost loss, forgot.

The Irish Americans started inviting us to their merry wakes, their funerals. It helped. To celebrate their life joyfully, be intimate with the body; to be playful at a wake, it worked for us to collectively remember why it was worth it to love them. Don't cry: it will keep the soul here. Laugh. Then, to watch a public performance of mourning—that helped, too. We could watch a woman keen, and it made us feel more pity and sorrow than if we were to cry. It purged us.

7

We knew the term catharsis was originally a medical term for the expelling of menstrual and reproductive fluids. What the body doesn't need anymore, to restore balance. We knew the term as the reason we turn to art, the reason why seeing someone else play out a tragedy helps us with our own. When the keener straightens her shoulders, lets us see her tears, then walks away, we follow her out of that space.

So, consensual reverse colonization—Ireland didn't impose their cultural customs on us, but they let us adopt them, those of us who no longer had any of our own.

But, of course, it doesn't totally work.

Maeve first gained her fame because she was beautiful, not because she was unattainable. We all could be her if we tried a little harder. We could never be Beyoncé, we knew that. No matter what we bought or who we hired to do our hair we could never be Janelle or Adele or Angelina or Andreja or Rihanna or Gaga or Jazz or Kim or Gwyneth (though we didn't really want to be Kim or Gwyneth anymore—but, of course, we still watched everything they did). But Maeve wasn't so styled; her skin didn't look so plastic. Maybe if we knew what mascara she used we could look so awake. Her arms were a touch plump, barely, so we could maybe accomplish her musculature with a bit of light lifting. And we understood that her talent was cultivated. She worked at it, so she felt like us, what we could be if we'd chosen to perfect a skill other than secretarial arts or how to draw blood from a five-year-old without tears or how to impeccably make a bed.

None of us could afford to hire her to mourn our dead. But we didn't resent her for that, either. Because we'd all seen her work, were all so moved when she channeled our grief over Prince, Bowie, Left Eye, Whitney... she set the bar so high that the keeners we did hire were excellent, had to be to stay in business— Siobhán from down the block was wonderful when Mr. Wilson died, and Sinéad was just as good when our grandmother passed. If we could hire Maeve McNamara, we would, just like when in junior high when we had extra babysitting money we bought Guess jeans because the triangle on our butts did make us feel cuter, even though our moms were right that jeans from Sears fit just as well. Maeve was out of our league, but not so much so that she made us feel bad about our keeners or our mom jeans or watching the royal wedding on television and not being invited. She made us happy in her sapphire fascinator. And when she keened for Brexit, we all felt a little better about that severing. Then when she keened for the end of the United Kingdom—Ireland reunited, Wales and Scotland independent, the Queen off all the money except in England, everyone else on the Euro—she knew without us having to tell her to make it a little bit jubilant, to allow a trill of possibility in her voice, to help us not feel too bad that a dynasty was dying. The modulation of sorrow and terror and love in her keening was sublime; she didn't need a production crew and lighting direction to perform; we knew that Givenchy for a rockstar's overdose was mailed to her apartment in Flatbush—she was good but she couldn't afford that—and the Versace for the last woman to die of an illegal abortion in Ireland was a gift; the suit she wore for Holly Woodlawn was given because the filth of the grave looks so good on Chanel.

While we wanted to be her, she didn't make us stop wanting to be ourselves.

The photo that appeared in the tabloids the next

day is of Maeve and Hungry laughing. They're at the after party at Le Bain, sitting near the pool, drinking champagne, and they look buoyant. The reporter had asked them if they were disappointed that the documentary Maeve appeared in didn't win, and she'd said no, the one that won was more artistic, more of an exploration than an explanation. "We don't need any more information," she said. "I was grateful to be a part of *Threnody*—I'm glad the film exists to show the history of mourning and how we got here—but I'm also glad a lesser-known director won." The reporter asked Hungry, "Why the bones?" and she answered, "We don't need more pretty queens." The reporter thanked them for their time and, after walking away, turned back to see them with heads upraised, throats exposed, uproarious. What she didn't hear them say, but one of us did, was Maeve telling Hungry, "I want to throw you in that pool so bad, see what you look like when all that slides off of you," and Hungry answered, "But you would never do that."

"No, I would never do that," Maeve said, and when they laughed, we saw the pleasant surprise of companionship and trust. They didn't hear the click of the shot.

Maeve said later she was pleased with the photo. She knew to mostly strike solemn poses for the cameras, but it was okay for the keener to be occasionally caught in an uncalculated moment of mirth. For people to see that she was still capable of that.

In the chat rooms, in our Facebook groups, in text chains with women in the neighborhood and across the nation, friends we'd made through our obsession, we imagined that the next morning she handed the rag to Hungry, along with a cup of coffee. He was just as lovely without makeup. He smiled at Maeve and said, "You are exquisite. And fierce. You'll be the one to keen Beyoncé someday."

Maeve would, of course, answer, "The Queen will never die."

We were pleased with the photo, too. We knew Maeve didn't date, instead had a string of one-night stands and hired escorts, but we were glad she and Hungry were enjoying each other. We all loved her a little, this woman no longer capable of love.

Maeve then became most famous for the ways she could channel her own tragedies—we knew all about all of them—into grief performances for others. She had few friends aside from her mother, Clare, named after the county in Ireland her grandparents had immigrated from. Her mother was retired now. Clare trained her daughter after Maeve's first keen, when she'd spontaneously joined her mother in mourning her father, who drowned in the Hudson River. Her mother's last keen was for Maeve's son, a stillbirth. After all of that, we understood Maeve to be untouchable.

Maeve told us the story in a profile with *Rolling Stone*. She'd never found the person she'd looked for her whole life, never felt that recognition of, *Oh, you. There you are.* She never found someone she wanted to belong to. So she found a person who would be a strong parent and partner and figured, *Let's do this.* She wanted to have a child because it was the only thing that made her hopeful, that the world would become good enough for her child to be in. She and Jake got pregnant quickly, and the pregnancy was hard, but no harder than any other.

Then the worst thing that could happen

happened.

Maeve recognized the scream right away. The banshee shrieked so many times Maeve yelled back at her, "Go away! Leave my home." The banshee gave her such a sad look, lifted the hood of her cloak, and was gone.

Maeve was sitting up in bed, Jake looking terrified. "It's either my mother or Cillian," she said. "I have no other relatives." She didn't know who she wished it wasn't. Then her water broke, and she knew.

She told Jake not to come to the hospital, and he said she knew he couldn't let her do this alone. He asked if she wanted him to call a taxi or an ambulance. Cillian wasn't moving, so she said ambulance, then stopped speaking.

Jake listened from the hallway.

It was as bad as it gets. Hours of labor knowing the child was already gone. She begged for them to knock her out, cut the child from her, please don't make her do this. They told her it was safer for her to deliver her child, and she told them to fuck themselves and let her die. *Please make this stop.* Her mother held her hand the entire time and said nothing because there was nothing to say.

When it was done Maeve held the body that was supposed to be Cillian, and she and her mother smiled at his beauty. He'd been dead for hours, his soul already on its way. Some things you can't merry wake, so Clare keened him, softly at first. Maeve closed her eyes and acknowledged that this had to happen. When she opened them to look at her son, her mother keened loudly enough that every room on every floor of the hospital could hear. The end of a lineage—she knew her daughter would never try again. The last McNamara. This child named for strife would never know pain or pleasure. Chláir ní Conmara, mother of Méabh ní Conmara, grandmother of Cillian mac Conmara, sounded that day like two boards being banged together, like an owl; she could have shattered glass: she channeled the ancients. All the mothers in all the other rooms shed silent tears for what they could have endured.

The grandmother's last keen.

That keen, of course, wasn't televised, but those who were there have told it and retold it so many times we all feel like we saw it. We remember this one because it showed us that some grief destroys us. But we don't die.

We were so grateful Maeve told us about what had happened to her. It made us feel like we knew her. She told us all of it.

After they'd cleaned and stitched her, Jake came in.

"You are so beautiful. And so strong."

"Thank you." Then, "I can never go back there."

"I know. I'll pack up your things. I'll give away the stuff in the nursery. I'll sell the apartment. I'll handle it."

"Thank you."

The room felt empty, even with both of them in it.

Jake said, "I am so sorry this happened to you."

The only thing there ever is to say to the face of grief.

Maeve was so grateful for his saying *you*, not *us*, that she gave it back to him. "I'm so sorry this happened to us."

And then he said the perfect thing. He ran his hand through his long wavy hair, looked at Maeve with the blue eyes she'd hoped her son would inherit, and

he said, "I am glad I got the chance to love you, Maeve."
Then, "If you ever need anything…"

"I know."

And then, with Maeve sweaty and distressed, with her still bleeding into the pad they'd put between her legs, on this, the worst day of her life, Jake did the perfect thing: he wound his hand in her dirty hair and kissed her, not holding back, one of the best kisses they ever shared. He kissed her as the woman she was to him and mother he knew she could be, and she was so grateful; then he said goodbye, and she never saw him again.

She said she thought of Cillian every day, and it never got easier.

That's when Maeve became world-renowned. That's when her vocal range expanded, and she became able to hit the note of a selkie who knows her pelt is locked away from her, the resonance of the old man at the pub who doesn't think the young college girl believes he saw a faerie in his garden when he was a child, the precise shriek of a banshee announcing the death of an O'Brien, the exact growl of a cornered cat, the hiss of a striking snake that never was on the island of Ireland for St. Patrick to remove. She could rumble at the timbre below human hearing of a mother whale seeking her lost calf, and our bones knew it even if our ears didn't; she became able to reach the pitch of every witch set aflame, the cries of a child touched by a priest, the wails of a man who knows no other way to enjoy desire, the tenor of a woman saying *no*, the tone of a hungry ghost begging to be saved or, at least, remembered, the weeping of a child who only knows her own language and can't express grief at the loss of her parents in English to the headmaster of the boarding school, the owl whose fledgling can't fly. When she hit that apex of unleashing, everyone listening knew that feeling too. Most of us had only seen her on television, but we'd heard that in person she was even more transcendent. When Maeve breathed and screamed to birth a child who would never breathe, she was connected to the lineage of all those who had loved and lost before her, all who had suffered. The more we love, the more we suffer. Their voices entered her lungs and her vocal chords, and her throat housed their stories and sang their griefs; she gave pain sound so the ones who loved the one now dead could stay silent. They let her do this for them, her voice giving movement to the letting go they all sought, the release.

This week, Maeve keened an unarmed Black teenager shot in the back in the street by police in Tennessee, a man electrocuted in Texas, a woman stoned to death in Somalia, a grandmother who died of heatstroke in New Orleans, and three teenagers shot by their classmate at school in Washington. At the end of a tough, typical week, she and Clare, who traveled with her everywhere, went to the hip-hop festival in Paris, featuring Childish Gambino, Kendrick Lamar, the Carters, Drake, Janelle Monáe, and, of course, Cardi B and Megan Thee Stallion. Damn. The pictures were marvelous—both Maeve and her mom threw their hands up in the air and sang along. Afterwards, eating fondue at a sidewalk café, on their second bottle of wine, Clare told the reporter, "What a great nod to the expatriated, to invite all those artists here. I wonder if any will just stay, say fuck going back to the States."

"I'm tempted to stay," Maeve said.

Her mother looked away from the press, looked to her daughter, said, "If you want to move, we can do that."

We loved how Clare always took Maeve seriously.

"I don't think that's what I really want. It's just nice to sometimes admit how tired I am."

We understood why Maeve was a workaholic—some kind of furious atonement, not for anything she herself did wrong, but just trying to heal somehow all the inflicted wounds. We were glad Clare never tried to talk her out of it. They just sat together in silence, in the presence of all the other conversations they'd had.

"Any last thoughts?" the reporter asked, a dashing man in an old-fashioned suit.

Maeve emptied her glass, said, "I miss James Baldwin."

"Oh man," her mom said. "Me too."

Fulaing. Áthas. Dorcadas.
Solas. Scrios. Buile. Nua.
Fulaing. Áthas. Dorcadas.
Solas. Scrios. Buile. Nua.
Fulaing. Áthas. Dorcadas.
Solas. Scrios. Buile. Nua.

CHAPTER TWO

Solas. Scrios. Buile. Nua.
Fulaing. Áthas. Dorcadas.
Solas. Scrios. Buile. Nua.
Fulaing. Áthas. Dorcadas.
Solas. Scrios. Buile. Nua.
Fulaing. Áthas. Dorcadas.
Solas. Scrios. Buile. Nua.

In her prime time interview, Oprah just dove right in, asking, "When did you know you wanted to do this? Take on the profession of mourning?"

"That's a long story," Maeve said.

"Tell it," Oprah enthused.

When Maeve started her period when she was thirteen, her mother was so excited to tell her father. "He'll be so proud that you're a woman now."

Maeve didn't think bleeding, or being able to produce offspring, was what made someone a woman. Or having ovaries and lining to slough off or even a vagina or vulva. Maeve thought it odd that in Irish *bean* means both woman and wife. As if a person who is one will naturally be the other as well. But Maeve accepted that her mom was old-fashioned—only women could be keeners, so becoming a woman was important. It was always assumed Maeve would take on the family business. Now, she could. Her mom didn't know many transwomen and nonbinary people like Maeve did, but Maeve thought her mother would accept anyone saying they were a woman, whatever their anatomy.

But before her mother could tell her father, the McNamara family banshee visited, right before Kieran was supposed to be home from fishing. Clare was cooking dinner, and Maeve was doing calculus homework at the kitchen table in blue pen—she was good at math—and thinking about Yahaira, wondering if she wanted to kiss Maeve as much as Maeve wanted to kiss her.

Then a scream made her mother drop the pot she was filling with water.

Their banshee was old and beautiful, with dark hair gone silver. Maeve had never met her. She shrieked again, then pulled up the hood of her chartreuse cloak and was gone.

Clare's hand was at her mouth, and she let it drop, as if embarrassed by her own shock.

Maeve said it. "Dad?"

"I don't know who else it could be."

They were grateful for the warning because it took a week to find the body. He'd worn the McNamara weave of Aran sweater, so they'd know it was him when he was found. The body couldn't be laid out for a merry wake, but they had one with his ashes. Maeve would be surprised if no one poured a little poitín into the urn. Her mother let her smoke one clay pipe and drink one glass of uisce beatha, but didn't know, though she wouldn't have cared, that it made Maeve bold enough to ask Yahaira if she wanted to get fake married. A boy from another school performed as the priest, and then they went into Maeve's bathroom because it had a door that locked. Their marriage was over at daylight, but they always smiled at each other at school. Maeve wondered if she should feel bad for having fun at her father's wake, but she didn't. That was the point, even when the dead were kin. She decided back then that at the next wake, she'd marry a boy for the night.

There was no way to pretend it was a fishing accident, so they didn't. They held the funeral at their home since there would be no burial, and that's where his ashes would stay. Their house was full, and the custom was to hire another keener so her mother wouldn't have to grieve; but she didn't trust anyone else to do it right.

Her mother howled, "Ciarán mac Conmara, son

of a sea hound, son of a seal, you have returned to the
water that was once your home."

Maeve surprised herself by standing and adding,
"We are sorry you were so lonesome on land."

Her mother also looked surprised, but Maeve
thought maybe also a little impressed, so Maeve felt
given permission to continue.

"We'd hoped to make you happy with us, but we
know you had to go home."

Maeve told Oprah that people said she was
gorgeous and precocious, but in the moment she just
felt calm. Even when they shifted into hysterics, it felt
right. Her higher-pitched voice harmonized with her
mother and made them sound like ten women. She'd
never seen it done before, but when her mother pulled
out a lock of black and white hair, Maeve yanked a hunk
of her own, and the pain made her gasp but in a good
way. Her father was supposed to be in a coffin, laid on a
table so she could see his face, and when she pictured
it in her mind, her voice rose higher. Her mother
screamed, "Why have you left us alone?" and before she
quite finished her note, Maeve sang over her, "We release
you," and they both dropped into a stunned silence; and
they were done.

We remember this one because it taught us
that some grief is formative, will forever shape who we
become.

Maeve decided to end the story she told Oprah
on a bit of joy. At Yahaira's cousin's merry wake, Maeve
got fake married to Dylan, and Yahaira performed the
ceremony, a double sacrilege to have a female priest,
and she smiled so slyly at Maeve. Yahaira lent them her
bedroom.

Maeve liked smiling at Dylan at school in the weeks after. When she ran into Yahaira in the bathroom she said, "I'm really sorry about your cousin."

"Thanks. Me too." Then, "How was it?"

"Fun. He's not as good as you are, but he's good enough."

Yahaira laughed.

And so, from the beginning, Eros and Thanatos, right next to each other.

We ate it up. It was so satisfying to hear about a kid becoming an adult whose exploits were less awkward than ours. (It never occurred to us that she maybe just left out the awkward parts on national television.) We wished we could have strutted like her when we were teenagers.

Our triumphs happened in private, hers were public.

But our humiliations were private too.

Adult Maeve didn't tell Oprah what we all already knew, had already seen, about what happened after— teenage Maeve being herded by paparazzi, shoved by reporters, terrorized by celebrity. She told the story of the beginning of her career, before the world knew who she was, before pictures of her inelegantly leaving a limo in a dress without underwear or trashed at a club would sell for millions, a time when she didn't yet know what it meant to always have to perform. She didn't yet know that we would turn on her if she didn't do exactly what we wanted; she didn't yet know that our appetite for titillation was insatiable; she didn't yet know how much money there was to be made from her suffering.

She gave us everything in her interview, and we always wanted more.

Teen Vogue was the mag to finally ask about her dad. Did she miss him? Yes, every day. Was she angry at him for leaving her? No. Asking him to be miserable so she wouldn't have to miss him wasn't fair.

Was she upset that she wasn't enough for him?

Of course. But she did all she could, and he did all he could.

"I think my dad had a touch of fey blood. He ever quite fit here. The story goes that our family name, McNamara, mac Conmara in Irish, means son of a sea hound, son of a seal. The idea is that our family was begun by a selkie and a mortal. Selkies are seals that discard their pelts on land and become humans. They're always very beautiful. If someone steals their pelt and keeps it away from them, they can't return to the sea. Many mortals have married selkies in their human form, and hid their pelt to keep them. My mom and dad were quite happy; I think mom kept him around a lot longer than he would have stayed otherwise. They met in college and said they just knew. They were married after three months. Together for eighteen years. But dad always had this lonely way about him. Not at all that mom trapped him and kept him with us, but just this longing, like there was something he wanted and never found. Like he belonged in a place he never could find. Love ended up not being enough to keep him here."

"And you've accepted that?"

"I don't think any person is powerful enough to really fix someone else. We all have to find a way to be complete, without anyone else, whether or not we find love. That's what I want your readers to know, all the young women who maybe think only love matters. It can matter, a lot. But it's only part of life, and it's up to us to live the life we want, with or without a partner."

Teen girls wrote her fan mail all the time, told her

she helped them heal when Cory Monteith died, and Amy Winehouse, and Alan Rickman—because they saw someone just as sad as they were, but who knew how to say it. They felt validated in their sorrow, articulated. But after this interview they started to write to tell her that they were trying to be complete in themselves, with or without finding their soulmate. Their words.

The day after the Oscars, the day after taking Hungry home, the day of the picture of her laughing appearing in the tabloids, the banshee returned. This time, she didn't even wail. She just touched Maeve's shoulder, and said, "I'm so sorry."

Maeve took a breath, about to cry, and the banshee said, "No. Her soul is traveling. You can't. You know what you have to do."

Maeve said, "Please don't make me do this," and the banshee answered, "You know we have no choice." Then, "You are strong enough to endure even this, Méabh ní Conmara."

Then, "At least you will never have to see me again."

The banshee looked older, weary. Maeve didn't get a chance to ask what would happen to her, now that all the McNamaras' deaths had been foretold, no one left to tell before Maeve's death. She lifted her cloak and was gone.

She got the call three long hours later. Her mother dead. Heart attack at sixty. Found in Maeve's childhood home in Hell's Kitchen. Would she like to place an order with Amazon for the merry wake supplies? Yes, yes she would.

Fulaing. Áthas. Dorcadas.
Solas. Scrios. Buile. Nua.
Fulaing. Áthas. Dorcadas.
Solas. Scrios. Buile. Nua.
Fulaing. Áthas. Dorcadas.
Solas. Scrios. Buile. Nua.

CHAPTER THREE

Solas. Scrios. Buile. Nua.
Fulaing. Áthas. Dorcadas.
Solas. Scrios. Buile. Nua.
Fulaing. Áthas. Dorcadas.
Solas. Scrios. Buile. Nua.
Fulaing. Áthas. Dorcadas.
Solas. Scrios. Buile. Nua.

Maeve's friend Nymph was the one to be with her after and told all the tabloids all about what happened that day, after Maeve got the news.

Nymph told us that Maeve always told her everything, so we trusted her version.

Would Maeve keen her mother? The question made her want to quit. To never keen again. To run away, but to where she didn't know.

Maeve sat in her kitchen drinking coffee in the afternoon. She remembered being a child, when the most comforting space in her universe was against her mother. Her mother's smell that wasn't from perfume, but somehow her essence made manifest—soap and detergent and her atoms mixing to make Maeve's knowledge of home. Her mother held her hand on the worst day of her life and then sang Maeve's grief into vibrations she still felt. If it weren't for her mother, she would have killed herself after Cillian died. Maeve thought of all the times she stood alongside her mother, keening the dead, mourning the lost, and in those moments, Maeve felt significant and meaningful and as whole as she ever felt. She'd keened alone since her mother retired, since Cillian died, but she always had her mother at her side. Clare took her to buy clothes when she was a teenager and managed to make her feel *pretty*, for Christ's sake. And now Maeve was alone.

Maeve poured her coffee down the drain, poured herself a bourbon neat, and sat back down.

She thought, *What would make me feel better?* As always, there were only two answers—*Talk to my mom, and have someone fuck my brains out.*

She poured her whiskey down her throat, put her hair in a messy bun, put on deodorant and a fresh pair of panties, put back on the jeans and t-shirt she'd been in, put on her nude Manolo Blahniks, and called a Hyper to go see Nymph.

She'd originally picked Nymph for her stage name—the mythological creature who mated with men and women at will, out of the control of men or gods, the root of Freud's term for a psychological disorder: women who liked sex too much. Maeve adored Nymph because she was irreverent, hilarious, and very attentive.

Maeve stepped into her cab, and the driver said, "Hey, you're that keener." Maeve said she was. "Will you do the funeral for those Asian women that got shot up in their spa?"

"I hope so. I haven't heard from their families, I'm sure they're trying to decide what on earth they want to do, but I'd like to help if I can."

"That's good," the driver said. He had a light Caribbean accent. "What you do, it does help."

"Thank you," Maeve said, trying to control the wavering in her voice. "I hope it does. But I always wish I could do more."

"Like stop dudes from murdering women?"

"Well, yeah."

The cabbie pulled up to the address, realized where he was, and said, "Oh." Approvingly. Maeve tipped him and rated him on her phone, stepped out, and he said, "Have fun."

Maeve almost said, *I will*. She paused. She said, "I'll try."

She walked into the strip club and Eros and Thanatos were on stage. Maeve loved watching them dance. They looked so similar, but moved so differently. Their dance was a seduction and a fight. Both were

26

wearing red today.

Nymph found Maeve and handed her a bourbon, then sat. Maeve reached out and held her hand and watched. Eros moving slow and balletic with Thanatos's hand at her throat.

In the pause between acts, Nymph asked, "How are you?"

Maeve smiled. "Not good."

Maeve told her all about it.

Nymph asked, "Do you know what would help?"

"Not today."

"I'll help you figure it out. Do you want to go in the back room?"

Maeve nodded. She wanted nothing more. In fact, she wanted nothing else. She could think of no other single thing she wanted. That she could have.

She followed Nymph to a back room, asked her to cover the mirrors. Nymph pulled black curtains across the walls, dimming the reflected light.

Nymph looked at her. "Would you like me to cut your hair?"

Again, Maeve nearly cried. She nodded.

Nymph went into the back room and brought out a basin of steaming water, a towel, shampoo, conditioner, and scissors. She had Maeve lay on the ground, and she very gently washed her hair, rubbing suds into her scalp, massaging her temples and her neck, bringing her wet hands down to Maeve's shoulders and digging into the tension. Maeve felt herself relax. The pads of Nymph's fingers circled and circled Maeve's muscles, deep in Maeve's curls. The shampoo smelled like oranges.

Nymph replaced the water and rinsed Maeve's hair, then conditioned it, then rinsed again. The conditioner smelled like tea tree oil. Nymph sat Maeve in a chair feeling steamy and relaxed. She fed her whiskey, then used scissors to shear her locks. Maeve didn't care what she did to her. Her head felt lighter and lighter.

When Nymph was done, she asked, "Do you want to see?" Maeve said no.

So then Nymph tied a blindfold around Maeve's eyes, and both cleaved and filled her. Maeve unclenched.

They lay on the ground kissing, and Maeve said, "Thank you," then paid her.

"Of course," Nymph said. "Anytime, sweetheart. And thank you."

They'd talked before about how a job was a job; sometimes it was satisfying, sometimes it was drudgery, but some of their clients they really enjoyed. If Maeve were a different kind of person, she would have tried to date Nymph.

"I can't do it," Maeve said. "I cannot keen my mother."

We always knew it would be the keeners' hearts that would give out.

That poor girl.

Then we wondered how this would change her voice.

Maeve borrowed a pair of sneakers from Nymph, and they walked home together in silence. RSVPs were coming in for the wake, and she saw that her package was delivered. Her mother's body would be there in an hour. She was having the wake at her apartment instead of her mother's home because she wanted her mother in her home one more time. The clouds were cracking the sun's rays into the spectrum. The lights on the Brooklyn Bridge were turned on, though they didn't need to be yet. As the Manhattan Bridge descended into Chinatown, Maeve smiled at the graffiti, the clotheslines, the water towers, the East River shining the sun's reflected rays bright as the moon, the people walking below her with produce in orange plastic bags, the people walking alongside her with headphones and dogs and flowers, the azure sky just beginning to fade to indigo, the sun on her skin. Nymph took her hand.

Maeve showered, put on her father's sweater, jeans, no makeup. Nymph helped her carry seven boxes up the stairs then unpack clay pipes, tobacco, uisce beatha, white cloth, and twine to tie her mother's big toes together. She unpacked the glass votives, the wake cakes and soda bread, the ham and lamb and jam and butter, the salted cod and herrings and nettle champ and bacon boxty, the black and white blood puddings, the crubeens and cut-and-come kale, boiled butter eggs and periwinkles and oysters. The stout and the tea.

Then the men from the morgue laid her mother's body on the kitchen table that Maeve and Nymph had dragged into the living room. The men took their plastic bag back with them. Her mother was naked and very thin. Nymph asked if she should leave, and Maeve said she could stay. It was nice to have a witness. *If* this was something that Nymph could hold with her, and she said she could. Maeve filled a basin with hot water and bathed her mother. She cleaned between her fingers, between her toes, the crease where her legs met her hips, her inner elbows. Maeve used her fingers to untangle her mother's curls, then washed her face, her earlobes, her lips, her eyebrows, her jawline. Maeve knew she wasn't as beautiful as her mother. She pictured her, seventeen years ago, washing the body of Maeve's father while Maeve watched. Maeve had her mom's eyes, and her dad's chin. She ran her white washcloth over her mother's clavicles, tied her toes together, still painted lavender, and then wrapped her mother's strong, fragile body in white fabric.

Maeve was made inside of this body.

She wrapped her arms around her own stomach, and her buzzer rang.

The first guests were families who'd hired her mother—Clare was never nearly as famous as Maeve—come to pay their respects. Maeve played the host, offering clay pipes to everyone, handing out glasses, thanking them for their sympathy, pointing out the spread of food. Soon, there were too many people for her to offer everyone a pipe herself, but they all knew what to do. She didn't get a plate of food because there were so many people to hug, but Nymph kept close by, kept her glass from getting empty.

She didn't know any of these people, really. Most she recognized.

Someone Maeve didn't recognize said, "I'm so sorry about your mother." Nymph hovered.

"This is my friend," Maeve said, lifting her chin. "She takes care of me."

The stranger nodded.

"Thank you for your condolences. How did you know my mother?"

The young woman smoked a clay pipe like she was born to it. "I knew of her. I wasn't born yet when she keened Kurt Cobain, but I've seen the film. I wouldn't have made it through Maynard James Keenan's death without her. And you, of course, you'd joined her by then."

"I still miss Maynard," Maeve said.

"Me too." The young woman smiled, and even though it was a sad smile, it made her face lovely. She must have started listening to Tool when she was twelve—she couldn't be but about eighteen. Then she said, "Your mother, and you… you showed me what I want to do with my life."

"You want to be a keening woman?" Maeve had never met an aspiring professional mourner.

"Yes. I am sorry to intrude upon your grief, but I knew no other way to meet you. Méabh ní Conmara, Daughter of Chláir Nic an Airchinnigh, Bean Mhic Conmara, mother of Ciarán Mac Conmara, I want you to train me."

"Even though I want to quit?"

"Train me and you can."

"And you are?"

"Aibhlinn ní Shuilleabhán."

Maeve sized up Evelyn O'Sullivan. Ropey arms, glowing brown skin, natural hair just barely tinged red. "You Irish?" she asked.

"My father was. My mother was Jamaican. Another country colonized by England." This time she smiled for real. Young, but clever.

"Was?"

Nymph handed her a glass of whiskey.

"Thank you. Sláinte. When I became Evelyn instead of Evan they didn't understand."

"I see."

"They said they grieved the loss of their son. Please believe me, I have always been a woman."

"You don't need to convince me." Maeve drank. "I *actually* mourned a son. A child. Who died. I never got to know who they really were. Your parents are despicable." Maeve saw Cillian in her mind, taller than she, blue eyes and black hair; then she saw a daughter, and all she wanted was to put her arms around her, feel her chest rise and fall.

"Thank you for saying that," Evelyn said. She let the pain be there on her face, didn't try to hide it.

Maeve asked, "Do you think the world is ready for a biracial trans keener?"

"I would like nothing more than to find out. It would be an honor."

Evelyn looked to Nymph, who gently shook her head. No, she wouldn't tell anyone. So we never knew that Evelyn was trans, until after her death, when Maeve published her journals. For posterity.

Nymph picked up the story here. Maeve looked at the candles glinting in the smoky room, lit emerald and crimson and cobalt and gold. She took Evelyn's pipe and smoked it, because she didn't want to walk away to get her own just yet. The room started singing "There's Whiskey in the Jar." Maeve didn't say anything for a minute, so Evelyn went and filled a plate, then walked back and handed it to Maeve.

"If you give me this opportunity, I will strive to become essential. To you, and to the profession."

Maeve looked at her mother, wishing for her to rise from the table. Later tonight, the fine boys would likely rig her with wires to sit up and startle everyone waiting the vigil. The best wakes had that prank.

She ate an oyster while Evelyn waited patiently. She loved the taste of the sea. Finally, she said, "They'll be waking my mother for the traditional three days. But I can't stay. I fly to London tonight, to wake Queen Elizabeth in the morning, and Jodie Harsh that night."

"Oh shit. Jodie died?"

"Yeah."

"That sucks."

"Yeah. He was rad. Then I come back here, to keen Anthony Bourdain, then mom." Huh. She said it. "Or, I don't know, be at her keen." Evelyn didn't question what that obviously meant, that Maeve may not do it.

Instead, Evelyn said, "I thought they'd use you for Tony."

"Thank you," Maeve answered. Then, "You're welcome to join me and watch. See the whole process, not just what they show on television."

Evelyn's whole body relaxed. "Thank you for trusting me."

"I haven't yet agreed to train you. So far, I've only agreed to let you keep me company. Normally, my mom would travel with me. Go home and pack your best black clothes." She looked at Evelyn's formal jumper, boat-neck and quarter-sleeved. "That's nice. Do you have anything else? Just so you don't have to wear the same thing every day?"

"Of course. I'm a bartender. Everything I own is black."

"Can someone cover your shifts?"

"Certainly."

"Don't quit your job yet, okay?"

Evelyn paused. "Okay. I won't. Yet."

"Do you have a hat for the Queen?"

"I do not."

"We'll have time to go to a milliner's. I'll buy your plane tickets. Can you be back here in two hours?"

"I live in The Bronx. But yes." Evelyn looked excited and terrified. Good. Maeve didn't want her giddy.

Evelyn reached out her hand, and they shook. As she left, a man who'd been waiting patiently approached Maeve.

"Sean from McSorley's," he said. "Your mom and you keened Tommy Nolan. I'll never forget you for it. Is there anyone you'd like to marry tonight? Some are wanting to get started."

"I am much too old for that foolishness. But thank you for asking, Sean. I still miss Tom."

"Me too. He was a good man."

"Aida and Donovan have been eying each other. They're old enough, I'd say. Tell them they can use my room if they clean up. Any others who want can find a space."

He nodded. Maeve ate another oyster. She couldn't stomach anything else. Nymph filled her glass, said, "Consider this being your last one, love." The room started signing "Dirty Old Town," Shane MacGowan leading. He winked at her. She couldn't believe that guy was still alive. Boys were wrestling, nearly knocking over the table, as was the custom. The woman who did her mother's nails was drunk, as was the custom. Everyone should be soon. Maeve looked through the haze and wished her mother could see this.

Maeve told the wake she had to work, but thank you for keeping watch.

She went into her office and researched the Queen's lineage on her laptop while Nymph massaged her shoulders. This was the first keen she'd need notes for. Those royals kept good records. She typed the lineage on her peacock Olivetti Studio 45 and put the paper in the pocket of her carryon.

She heard "Finnegan's Wake" coming from her living room:

"… The liquor scattered over Tim
Tim revives, see how he rises
Timothy rising from the bed
Whirl your whiskey around like blazes
Tonamondeal, do you think I'm dead?
And whack Fol-De-Dah now dance to your partner
Welt the floor, your trotters shake
Wasn't it the truth I told you
Lots of fun at Finnegan's wake."

And to Maeve's surprise, she smiled. She hoped someone was sprinkling whiskey on her mom, just in case.

Fulaing. Áthas. Dorcaḋas.
Solas. Scrios. Buile. Nua.
Fulaing. Áthas. Dorcaḋas.
Solas. Scrios. Buile. Nua.
Fulaing. Áthas. Dorcaḋas.
Solas. Scrios. Buile. Nua.

CHAPTER FOUR

Solas. Scrios. Buile. Nua.
Fulaing. Áthas. Dorcaḋas.
Solas. Scrios. Buile. Nua.
Fulaing. Áthas. Dorcaḋas.
Solas. Scrios. Buile. Nua.
Fulaing. Áthas. Dorcaḋas.
Solas. Scrios. Buile. Nua.

Three days ago, Maeve's cell phone had rung from an international number, so she picked up. "The Queen died," a voice told her. "She would like you to keen her."

"Oh my god. I thought she'd never die."

"She was in her nineties?"

"Oh my god, you mean the Queen of England? I thought you meant Beyoncé."

The voice laughed, seemingly trying not to. "Americans. Are you free?"

"Of course. Forgive my mistake. It would be an honor to keen for Her Majesty. I am so sorry for your loss."

"Thank you. I'll email details straightaway."

One of us was on their plane and told us that Maeve and Evelyn slept the entire time, possibly drugged, and awoke in England. A shop girl at Rachel Trevor-Morgan's store told us that they arrived by cab, and Evelyn chose a black fascinator with feathers and flowers and a small veil. It was bold, but not flamboyant, and Maeve approved. She'd brought her wide-brimmed Phillip Treacy. The next taxi driver told us that in the cab, they strategized.

"I've met Kate and William before. Monarchy was a stupid governing system that I'm glad we got rid of, but they're lovely people. I've not met Meghan and Harry except at their wedding, so I don't really know them; but, of course, I think they're totally rad. Charles' coronation has been canceled, so I'm assuming he's the one now who will need the most consoling."

"How do you decide how sad to sound?" Evelyn asked.

"Part of it is planned. I mean, she lived a really long, good life. So medium-sad? But I'll feel out the family and get a sense of how her subjects are feeling, adjust. Some people who didn't know her at all totally loved her. So. I'll try to acknowledge that? And then a lot of it is just instinct."

"Okay. Thanks." Evelyn looked calm except that her fingers were all tangled together.

They met at Kate and William's apartment at Kensington Palace. Maeve walked in beaming, but the couple was unexpectedly frosty. Not sorrowful. Annoyed.

They all stiffly shook hands as Maeve introduced Evelyn as someone she might train, and Evelyn was polite and not overtly starstruck. "I am so sorry about your loss," she said to each. "I am sure you will miss her so much."

Kate looked at Maeve and said, "Not everyone wants you here, keener, and we didn't expect two."

William stayed stone-faced.

Evelyn looked at Maeve like, *What do we do?*

Maeve opened her eyes wide, like a shrug.

Then Charles walked in and surprised Maeve by hugging her. "I heard you just lost your mother, too." His voice hitched.

"I did," she said. "I am so sorry for your loss. I understand it."

"We're orphans," he said, and hugged her again.

She didn't ask if he was sad that he would not be king. No one asked that.

Harry and Meghan arrived, he in his black uniform and she with wrists and knees covered. They were cordial, but distant. They said they'd take Maeve and Evelyn in their car to Westminster Abbey. Then everyone would follow the sailors from the Royal Navy as they drew the gun carriage bearing the coffin to

Paddington Station, and they would all travel by train to Saint George's Chapel in Windsor Castle. This was a complicated one.

At first, the car was cloyingly silent. Then Harry said, "Sorry for the reaction you probably got from my brother."

"I'm guessing your publicist thought it best to hire me for propriety's sake, because the subjects would want their ruler honored by the biggest celebrity possible? But that's not what your family wants?"

"Right." After a pause, he said, "I mean, you keened Brexit. An Irish custom for the last of the United Kingdom?" Maeve couldn't read his tone.

"Clearly, I think it's perfect," Meghan said.

"I mean, you had flowers from all 53 commonwealths sewn into your wedding veil. I thought that was so badass," Maeve said.

"Thank you for noticing that," Meghan said.

"And… you left," added Evelyn. "Like, can we just state the obvious?" Maeve opened her eyes wide again, but Evelyn went on, "Also, you each were so great in that Oprah interview. You were so poised and vulnerable and graceful," she said to Meghan. "And Harry, you were a fucking furious and fierce partner."

Meghan visibly relaxed. Maeve admired Evelyn's grace and charisma. *Well played*, she mouthed. Evelyn gave a small nod.

Meghan shrugged. "Yeah. Thank you. They don't love that I'm here, either. And I'm sure the family was not pleased to see another Black woman show up, to, you know, emphasize me. As if I can ever not be emphasized."

Meg and Evelyn smiled at each other.

"So, what do you want me to do?" Maeve asked.

Harry answered, "We carry out tradition. Because

sometimes we must. Just do your job and get out as quickly as you can."

We didn't think to wonder if Evelyn was thinking, *When must we?*

"Okay," Maeve said. Then she tried to get Harry to relax. "Can I ask how the wake was?"

"Really fun?" he said.

Maeve laughed. He'd always seemed like an excellent person to party with.

"John Lyndon came and did 'God Save the Queen'; Moz came and did 'The Queen Is Dead.' It was very cheeky, and very hilarious."

"Oh my god."

"I know. I'm so sorry you were waking your mom; I wish you could have seen it. Skepta did a cover of that Bobby Brown song, but as 'It's My Royal Prerogative.'"

"Oh my god."

"I know. Best, best wake."

We were so glad that Harry and Meg's driver was one of us.

After the long journey, they were ready to intern the Queen. The Lord Chamberlain broke his white stave of office and threw it into the vault to symbolize the end of his period of service to the late monarch. At that crack, Maeve began.

Her grief did not have the texture of a performance, did not have the false ring of a routine. Real sorrow shattered her voice. She howled a crescendo, she modulated murmured, and sobbed; she yelled to the rafters, she droned, hummed, crooned.

Maeve knew she had to do the entire lineage, everything that led to this, all that stops here. She reached into the pocket of her velvet Prada pencil skirt, one of the few she had that covered her knees, and pulled out her typed notes. The first lineage too long for her memory. The first lineage with ancestors back to the year 519. A fifteen-hundred-year-long family tree she had to sing. She breathed deep, and sang clearly, with enunciation, so that all the names she'd practiced the pronunciation of could be heard. She gave the heredity the regal, majestic, imperial tone she thought it deserved, without leaving out the inherently patriarchal, colonial inheritance. Everyone listened to every word.

"Today we mourn Elizabeth Alexandra Mary, Queen of England, former Queen of the United Kingdom of Great Britain and Northern Ireland and Her other Realms and Territories, former Head of the Commonwealth, Defender of the Faith. Dei Gratia Britanniarum Regnorumque Suorum Ceterorum Regina, Consortionis Populorum Princeps, Fidei Defensor. Daughter of Albert Frederick Arthur George and Elizabeth Angela Marguerite, King and Queen of the United Kingdom and the Dominions of the British Commonwealth, the last Emperor and Empress of India; granddaughter of George Frederick Ernest Albert and Victoria Mary Augusta Louise Olga Pauline Claudine Agnes, King and Queen of the United Kingdom and British Dominions; descended from Edward the Seventh and Alexandra of Denmark, King and Queen of the United Kingdom and British Dominions; descended from Victoria, Queen of the United Kingdom of Great Britain and Ireland, and Albert, Prince of Saxe-Coburg and Gotha and consort of the Queen; descended from Edward and Victoria of Saxe-Coburg-Saalfeld, Duke and Duchess of Kent and Strathearn; descended from George the Third and Charlotte of Mecklenburg-Strelitz, King and Queen of the United Kingdom of Great Britain and Ireland, King and Queen of Hanover; descended from Frederick and Augusta of Saxe-Gotha, Prince

and Princess of Wales; descended from George the
Second, Prince-Elector of the Holy Roman Empire, and
Caroline of Ansbach, King and Queen of Great Britain
and Ireland and Duke and Duchess of Brunswick-
Lüneburg; descended from George the First and Sophia
Dorothea of Celle, King and Queen of Great Britain
and Ireland; descended from Ernest Augustus and
Sophia of Hanover, Elector and Electress of Brunswick;
descended from Frederick the Fifth and Elizabeth,
Elector and Electress of Palatine and King and Queen
of Bohemia; descended from James the Fifth, King of
Scotland, and the First King of England and Ireland,
and Anne of Denmark, Queen of Scotland, England,
and Ireland; descended from Mary, Queen of Scots,
and Henry Stuart, Duke of Albany and Lord Darnley;
descended from James the Fifth of Scotland and Mary
of Guise, King and Queen of Scotland; descended from
James the Fourth of Scotland and Margaret Tudor,
King and Queen of England; descended from Henry
the Seventh, Lord of Ireland, and Elizabeth of York,
King and Queen of England; descended from Edmund
Tudor, 1ˢᵗ Earl of Richmond, and Margaret Beaufort,
Countess of Richmond and Derby; descended from
John Beaufort, 1ˢᵗ Duke of Somerset, and Margaret
Beauchamp of Bletsoe; descended from John Beaufort,
1ˢᵗ Earl of Somerset, and Margaret Holland, Countess of
Somerset; descended from John of Gaunt and Katherine
Swynford, Duke and Duchess of Lancaster; descended
from Edward the Third, Lord of Ireland, and Philippa
of Hainault, King and Queen of England; descended
from Edward the Second of Carnarvon, Lord of Ireland,
and Isabella of France, King and Queen of England;
descended from Edward Longshanks, Lord of Ireland,
and Eleanor of Castille, King and Queen of England;
descended from Henry the Third of Winchester, Lord

of Ireland and Duke of Aquitaine, and Eleanor of Provence, King and Queen of England; descended from John Lackland, Lord of Ireland, and Isabella of Angoulême, King and Queen of England; descended from Henry the Second, Count of Anjou, Maine, and Nantes, Duke of Normandy and Aquitaine, and Lord of Ireland, and Eleanor of Aquitaine, King and Queen of England; descended from Geoffrey Plantagenet, Count of Anjou, Maine, and Touraine, and Duke of Normandy, and Empress Matilda; descended from Henry the First and Matilda of Scotland, King and Queen of England; descended from William the Conqueror and Matilda of Flanders, King and Queen of England and Duke and Duchess of Normandy; descended from Malcolm the Third and Margaret of Scotland, King and Queen of Scots; descended from Edward Ætheling and Agatha; descended from Edmund Ironside and Ealdgyth, King and Queen of England; descended from Æthelred and Ælfgifu of York, King and Queen of the English; descended from Edgar and Ælfthryth, King and Queen of the English; descended from Edmund and Ælfgifu of Shaftesbury, King and Queen of the English; descended from Edward and Eadgifu of Kent, King and Queen of the Anglo-Saxons; descended from Alfred the Great and Ealhswith, King and Queen of Wessex; descended from Æthelwulf, Noble Wolf, and Osburh, King and Queen of Wessex; descended from Ecgberht and *Redburga regis Francorum sororia,* the sister of the Frankish Emperor, King and Queen of Wessex; descended from Ealmund, King of Kent, wife unknown; descended from Eafa, Eoppa, Ingild, Cenred, Ceowald, Cuthwulf, Cuthwine; descended from Ceawlin, King of Wessex; descended from Cynric, King of Wessex; and descended from Cerdic, founder and first King of Saxon Wessex, all wives unknown."

People were smiling. "The House of Windsor lives on. The Houses of Hanover, Stuart, Tudor, Lancaster, Plantagenet, and Wessex live on in the descendants. The lineage continues, lives on in Charles, Andrew, Edward, and Anne; in William, Kate, George, Charlotte, and Louis; in Harry, Meghan, Archie, and Lilibet; in Beatrice and Eugenie; in James and Louise; in Peter and Zara; in Savannah and Isla; in Mia; and in all the descendants of Margaret, Henry, and George. Her Majesty, Her Royal Highness, Commander-in-Chief, woman of grace, poise, and elegance, we will miss your governance and your guidance."

She sounded like a symphony.

Everyone watched this one. And we remember it because of the pomp and circumstance. Because we realized that the ritual of grief always matters, but who deserves a performance and who doesn't is not agreed upon.

We knew the House of Bolkiah, the House of Wangchuck, the House of Bourbon, the House of Khalifa, the House of Hashim, the House of Al Thani, the House of Saud, the Alouite dynasty, the Luxembourg Grand Ducal Family, the Monegasque Princely Family, and the entire Zulu Royal Family were there. We wondered who everyone was going to try to set King Norodom Sihamoni up with. We were happy to see that Crown Princess Victoria, Prince Oscar, Prince Daniel, and Princess Estelle could all make it from Sweden. King Willem-Alexander and Queen Maxima of the Netherlands came with all their daughters, Princesses Amalia, Alexia, and Ariane. Only King Bhumibol Adulyadej and Princess Siribhachudabhorn could make it from Thailand, but we understood. Princess Astrid represented the entire Norwegian Royal Family herself, and we wondered at that.

Papers in the U.S. were delighted that Maeve made the Queen so clearly noble and phony. The House of Windsor never really ruled, and the Houses of Hanover, Stuart, Tudor, Lancaster, Plantagenet, and Wessex often ruled through bloodshed as much as bloodline. And that shift away from the titles when she listed The Queen's living relatives was such a simple, elegant way to indicate the end of an era, the end of a reign. Twitter had a field day.

The first person to speak to Maeve when she walked off stage was Evelyn. "That was epic," she said with a wide, gorgeous grin, her face turned toward Maeve and down so that no one else could see.

Maeve was exhausted. But that delighted her enough that she managed a small laugh in response.

Fulaing. Áthas. Dorcadas
Solas. Scrios. Buile. Nua.
Fulaing. Áthas. Dorcadas
Solas. Scrios. Buile. Nua.
Fulaing. Áthas. Dorcadas
Solas. Scrios. Buile. Nua.

CHAPTER FIVE

Solas. Scrios. Buile. Nua.
Fulaing. Áthas. Dorcadas
Solas. Scrios. Buile. Nua.
Fulaing. Áthas. Dorcadas
Solas. Scrios. Buile. Nua.
Fulaing. Áthas. Dorcadas
Solas. Scrios. Buile. Nua.

Then we all switched from the BBC to MTV to watch Jodie Harsh's wake and funeral. Both were at Dollar Baby at Metropolis. He was laid out dressed in his work suit: black pants with fringe all down the side, iridescent peep-toe zippered Terry de Havilland booties, sheer tank-top and '80s-shouldered gold bomber jacket, swept-to-the-side lavender bouffant and bangs, spiky eyelashes and extreme cat eyeliner flips, red lips. After the service, his body was to be burned and kept in an urn in the DJ booth, where Carl Cox was spinning now.

A waiter handed the keener a neon cerulean cocktail, and she didn't ask what it was. She and Evelyn drank—they looked like electric blueberries—and noshed on some popcorn. Boy George and Amanda Lapore were singing "Do You Really Want to Hurt Me?"—he beautifully, she badly. RuPaul looked gorgeous and forlorn. The muscle boys were shirtless and the pretty boys were painted and the ladies covered the spectrum from dyke to femme and we were a little overwhelmed.

She'd changed into that tight black leather dress that Givenchy sent her years ago, saying he'd trust her to find the right occasion for it. It was low-cut and short and had buckles. Purple knee-high Doc Martens, the first color we'd ever seen her wear. Hungry swung by and said she looked lovely, and she hugged her and said, "I'm so sorry for your loss." Her face done all in shades and shines of black was stunning, and all she wore was a corset and boots. "Jodie would love that," Maeve said with a nod.

"Thanks."

Maeve took another drink; Evelyn declined a

second. The waiter told Maeve that her envelope was behind the bar for her to pick up after, and the wake ended and the funeral began.

It was almost like bride's side, groom's side at a wedding—Jay Clarke's friends at the bar, Jodie Harsh's friends in chairs throughout the rest of the room. Jodie's casket spray was orchids, oncidium and dendrobium and cymbidium arcing wildly, brazen and gorgeous, blooms like faces and mouths and genitals.

Maeve began. "Destroyer of stigmas, giver of zero fucks, master of dirty electro, maker of parties, innovator of cabaret, leader of Ibiza, ringleader of every circus, way-paver, confidence-giver, fan-girl of *Ab Fab*, mixer of Madonna, Beyoncé, and Cher, daughter of Michael Jackson and Pamela Anderson, daughter of Barbie and Bozo, daughter of Canterbury, Kent, darling of London and Spain, dancer, fashionista, East-Ender, artist, beauty, punk, boy, queen, gender-fuck, rager. You made the invisible feel more seen and known. You reminded us that Pride should be fun. You wanted to die on the dance floor, and expected to. Why have you been taken from us so soon?

"You taught us that we can be smart and protest and shout and learn and work during the week, but on Friday night we just want to be Dollar Baby for a few hours. You taught us how to put on and take off our work suits. You taught us about truth telling and fantasy, being present in reality and escaping. You presented, you performed, and you let us be us.

"Fuck the human who took you from us. Fuck the hate that allows some people to think other people don't deserve to exist. We are filled with rage, Jodie. We are filled with sorrow. We will miss you, so much. And we'll continue to fight hard and love hard and party hard, in your honor."

48

And everyone said, "Amen."

We remember this one because we learned that Maeve ran comfortably in circles we didn't. We would have to stretch more than we'd known in order to be her.

When we saw Maeve comforting Evelyn after, we realized Evelyn was wearing Maeve's dress that she'd keened MJK in. We all wished Maeve could have been a mother.

No one told us about their plane ride home.

Fulaing. Áthas. Dorcadas.
Solas. Scrios. Buile. Nua.
Fulaing. Áthas. Dorcadas.
Solas. Scrios. Buile. Nua.
Fulaing. Áthas. Dorcadas.
Solas. Scrios. Buile. Nua.

CHAPTER SIX

Solas. Scrios. Buile. Nua.
Fulaing. Áthas. Dorcadas.
Solas. Scrios. Buile. Nua.
Fulaing. Áthas. Dorcadas.
Solas. Scrios. Buile. Nua.
Fulaing. Áthas. Dorcadas.
Solas. Scrios. Buile. Nua.

Evelyn didn't give many interviews after she took over as the most famous keener in the world, but she did tell CNN about her walk with Maeve to keen Anthony Bourdain.

We wondered why Maeve didn't tell us about it herself.

Evelyn met Maeve at her apartment in Flatbush to walk to Brooklyn Fare. We knew Maeve liked to walk to any keens she could in New York to settle her mind, prepare. In Crown Heights, they talked about their favorite bagel joints and delis until Maeve stepped on a spot on the sidewalk and met a hungry ghost. She told Evelyn after that her first thought was, *I will die in this place.*

She said she tried to think through suffocating fear. *Where am I?* Brooklyn. *What neighborhood?* Crown Heights. *I know this. I learned this one. I know his name.*

She couldn't breathe. She couldn't hear me screaming at her.

Trayvon Martin. No. *Tamir Rice.* No. *Sandra Bland.* No. *Where am I?* Brooklyn. *Amadou Diallo.* No, the Bronx. *Stephon Clark, Alton Sterling.* No. Not here. *Michael Hansford.* No, the Bronx. She fought against the terror of not being able to make her lungs work. *George Floyd.* Not here. *Jacob Blake.* Alive. *Breonna Taylor.* Not here. *Brooklyn.* Finally, she was able to say, "Saheed Vassell," and was released.

I pulled her into me and said, "Oh my god. I didn't know we were on his block. Are you okay?"

Maeve was gasping. But breathing. She nodded.

A woman watching from the bodega across the way walked over and sat with us on the sidewalk. She wore a blue headscarf that matched her eyeshadow. "I know that's rough," she said, "but we don't mark it on purpose. We want people to meet him and remember."

I kept my hand on her back and said, "I always wonder about the Black people who were killed in their homes. In prisons. In their grandparents' backyard. Do you think the family just learns to walk around that spot?"

"I wonder that, too," the woman said.

"Or do they step on the spot once a day, every morning on their way to make the coffee? And say their name, say their name, say their name," Maeve said. She was sobbing.

The woman from the neighborhood smiled and told her, "You seem like a nice white lady. Or at least one who's trying to understand."

"I'm sure there are ways I'm a total asshole," she said with her face in her hands.

The woman nodded and went back to work.

Maeve shook her hands to sling the tension out, then held them level and saw she was trembling. Then she told me about her grandparents, who came to the U.S. from County Clare, which is why her parents named her mom that. They knew she'd lose the family name and banshee, McInerney, when she married, and they wanted her to always have a reminder of the county she came from. Maeve described their banshee as young and quiet, her portent washing bloody clothes, no matter the type of forthcoming death. She wore a red cloak and had bright red hair. She was terrifying, her mom said. When her grandparents emigrated, they family merry waked them, because they knew they'd never see them again.

Her grandfather told her when she was a kid that his father met a hungry ghost on a patch of hungry grass in County Clare. He had a bit of bread in his pocket, just in case, as everyone in Famine regions did, knowing how many died. So he got away. But he said it was awful.

"So I stood up, and I stepped on the patch of hungry asphalt, and I felt that suffocating fear, that loss of my breath, that sense of how unfair it was that I was about to die, and I waited as long as I could before I said Saheed Vassell."

Anderson Cooper couldn't hide his surprise. "Why did you do that?"

"Because I'm sure it will happen to me again, there are so many spots, and now I'll be better prepared when it happens and I'm not expecting it."

He asked, "As a woman of color, are you always preparing yourself for violence?"

"I'm not going to tell you about my life. You get my public persona, and nothing beyond that. Though, that you even have to ask speaks volumes." Evelyn didn't explain more about that. She just waited a beat, then said, "I can almost imagine a world without gender-based violence. Almost. But I cannot imagine a world without race-based violence."

We'd never thought about that before.

"I've never thought about that before," Anderson said.

"Because you don't have to. So, then Maeve held me until I stopped shaking; we asked each other if we were okay, then we walked to keen Tony. And you know all about that."

Anderson asked why there weren't hungry spots for every murdered slave.

"I've wondered that, too. It was literal hunger that brought the ghosts to Ireland, but the ghosts here have transformed to being figuratively hungry. I don't know what makes the ghosts come, but we're getting more and more haunted. I wonder if there will be eight ghosts inside of that spot of anti-Asian hate. I wonder who will find out."

We all watched Anthony Bourdain's merry wake and funeral on CNN and didn't learn what came before until later.

We knew Maeve liked to show up to the end of a wake, then process with the mourners to the cemetery, if that's what they chose to do. Part of her pay was food and booze, and she knew that family and friends liked to see that the keener was a human, before she launched into her sublime mania.

We'd never been to Brooklyn Fare, but we knew Maeve had been there once on a date; we knew, through her, how spectacular it was. Eric Ripert, Andrew Zimmern, Sean Brock, David Chang, Deuki Hong, Angela Dimayuga, Marcus Samuelson, Anthony's ex-wives and girlfriend and daughter, and probably a few others, had dinner there the night before, César Ramirez eating with them from behind the counter. Today, there was just going to be simple street food and cold beer. Celebrating all the sides of Tony.

We weren't surprised to see Anthony sitting up with a beer in his hand. Maeve wore black skinny jeans and a Ramones t-shirt and heels, and that was perfect. Rose McGowen was tending to Asia Argento, and Frances Bean was hugging Ariane. Evelyn looked a little starstruck in her New York Dolls t-shirt, like she wanted to meet everyone in the room, but was too shy to talk to anyone. All the chefs were there, nursing last night's near-certain debauchery with fried foods.

We watched Maeve eat an eggroll, a cabeza de vaca taco, chicken heart yakitori, a shot of ceviche.

"I never met him," she said to Evelyn, like she'd

suddenly realized.

Then his best friends put Tony in a box, and put the box on a trailer behind a motorcycle, and then taxis pulled up to take all the mourners to Green-Wood Cemetery.

For this funeral, there were no readings, no songs, just Maeve and then everyone would throw a handful of dirt on the coffin. She held the mic like she was in a metal band, and began. "We know you didn't want to leave us. You fought to be here… you didn't let the cocaine kill you; you didn't let the heroin kill you; you didn't let the methaqualone, secobarbital, tuinal, amphetamines, and codeine kill you. You quit cigarettes! You chose to live, and you let us watch you do it fully. You ate it all. You drank it all. You said it all and you saw it all. You woke to beautiful views nearly every morning of your life, but you woke alone. You said, 'Look at this beautiful lake. Why am I so lucky to see it? Okay, I've seen it. Now I want to dive into it and drown.' And now you have. You didn't want to see it anymore. You didn't leave a note. You had nothing left to say. And we are so bereft, left grieving your leaving, left missing all we loved about you."

"You told us to travel, and we did. You told us to share meals and learn about people though what they served, and we did. We ate anything they gave us. We wanted to be just like you. And then you didn't want to be you anymore. And we can't wish for you to stay here and suffer so that we don't have to miss you." Maeve was alternately yelling and whispering. "We wish you didn't suffer. We know you did everything you could. We did everything we could. You had it all and it wasn't enough. You drank it all down, ate it all up, and it was never, never enough. We wish you still wanted to be alive, Saint

Anthony The Opinionated, but you made us want to be more alive. You made us dream, you made us accomplish some of those dreams, we tried to be as fearless as you seemed."

"Some of us understand, some of us do not. Anthony Bourdain, son of Pierre and Gladys, father of Ariane, spouse of Nancy Putkoski and Ottavia Busia, lover of Asia Argento, friend to so many, why have you left us alone?

We will think of you when we eat bone marrow. Street tacos. Noodles from a food truck. We will think of you when we eat escargot, foie gras, steak tartare, and pommes frites, even though they're never as good anywhere else as they were at Brasserie Les Halles. When a man hands us a round of mozzarella he made himself, when we open a perfect tin of brined sardines, when we drink a beer alone in the afternoon in an Irish pub that is just fine, when we when we try calf brain for the first time, we will think of you. You showed us that all that fine French food is cooked by men from Mexico. You toasted La Raza. You chided us for being shocked at seeing Palestinian people's simple meals, simple hopes. You didn't drink in Iran. You advocated for the release of prisoners, and you counseled them when they were freed. You were a feminist, helped women be fierce, held yourself to a higher standard than everyone who disgusted you. Punk. Blue belt in jiu-jitsu. Emmy winner, Clio winner, Best Food Writer, Best Food Book, honorary Doctor of Humane Letters honoris causa in the Culinary Arts. You earned all the accolades.

Your lyricism. Your swagger. Your brilliance. Your generosity.

Renegade. Unapologetic. Passionate. When we learned you didn't come down for dinner, you didn't come down to breakfast, you wouldn't be filming at the market today, we sat on the ground.

You made us love the Waffle House, that "beacon of hope and salvation inviting the hungry, the lost, the seriously hammered, all across the South to come inside." You made us a little less afraid of the unknown. You made us feel more connected with our planet and people we will never meet. You taught us that our weird is the world's delicious.

You made us try things.

You made us try things.

We watched your show from space. We watched you eat sheep testicles in Morocco, ant eggs in Mexico, raw seal eye as part of Inuit tradition, the beating heart, blood, bile and meat of an entire cobra in Vietnam. We watched you eat unwashed warthog rectum in Namibia, fermented shark in Iceland, and Chicken McNuggets in New York. Nothing human was alien to you. You will always travel with us, Tony. You made us omnivorous, nomadic; we are ravenous, we are insatiable like you, but may we all want to stay."

For him, she tore out fingers full of strands of hair, tangled in her knuckles.

She screamed, screeched, and shrieked, and no one covered their ears.

We grieved his choice so hard, but Maeve helped us see it as a choice.

We remember this one because we knew that Maeve was really talking about herself the whole time.

Fulaing. Áthas. Dorcaðas
Solas. Scrios. Buile. Nua.
Fulaing. Áthas. Dorcaðas
Solas. Scrios. Buile. Nua.
Fulaing. Áthas. Dorcaðas
Solas. Scrios. Buile. Nua.

CHAPTER SEVEN

Solas. Scrios. Buile. Nua.
Fulaing. Áthas. Dorcaðas
Solas. Scrios. Buile. Nua.
Fulaing. Áthas. Dorcaðas
Solas. Scrios. Buile. Nua.
Fulaing. Áthas. Dorcaðas
Solas. Scrios. Buile. Nua.

These were the most important days of Maeve's career, the ones we paid the closest attention to. She was at the height of her fame, her powers. She was taking on this gravitas that was astounding to us all. We had no idea it was the end, that she was going to quit at her apex.

Maeve dyed her mother's wedding gown black. The only white thing her mother had owned, a gift from Vera Wang, custom designed as a thank-you for the beautiful keen of her grandmother. On Clare's wedding day, everyone was so happy to see the keener happy. The dress was lace, high-necked and cap-sleeved, mermaid cut, with a deep keyhole back. Dyed ebony it was spooky: and suited Maeve, how haunted and gaunt she looked these days.

People didn't cover the wedding at the time—Clare's fame didn't rate—but they asked Maeve about it when they interviewed her later. Maeve had studied pictures of her parents' wedding since she was old enough to understand that ceremony. They married outside in the sunshine underneath the Brooklyn Bridge, Manhattan spread before them, her mother barefoot in couture, her father in a white suit with a ribbon tied round his neck. Her mother carried a handful of orchids, and she'd put one in her groom's buttonhole.

"It was the happiest day of my life," her father told her. "The second-happiest day was the day you were born," he said with a warm smile. Then, "Maeve, I'm sorry, I probably shouldn't have told you that."

Maeve answered, "Dad, it's totally fine if you love

mom more than me." She was ten.

"No, it's not that at all." He seemed genuinely distressed.

"I can imagine watching someone give birth would be really harrowing." Maeve was the kind of ten-year-old who knew words like harrowing. "I think if I ever have a kid it will be interesting and exciting. But I can't imagine it would primarily be a happy day. It's the beginning of something, the day you met me. But a wedding, the public ritual of it, the ceremonial aspect, it's the beginning of something, too, but it's also the consummation of what's come before. And an aesthetic collaboration. If I ever get married, I want it to be the prettiest day of my life and totally the happiest."

Her dad listened to her with awe and joy. "You'll make a really incredible keener," he told her. "You get stuff."

"Thanks, Dad."

Then he asked her if she wanted to get married, if she wanted to have kids. She answered "yes" to both confidently, but she said that she wondered now if at ten she just hadn't seen any other model for how to live, yet. It seemed like the only life to have. At thirty, Maeve had given up. She didn't know if she still wanted them or not, because it didn't matter.

After the keen for her mother, Maeve was interviewed by *People* again.

She never decided to keen her mother, never hired anyone else; then the decision was made. Her mother was radiant and helped people, so to Maeve she was hyperreal, superhuman, a goddess, abundant. And she listened to Maeve as if nothing she said could ever be wrong, like she could hold anything.

That kind of attention meant that she asked

Maeve the question this way: "Are there any boy or girls you like at school?" When Maeve answered, with glee, "There are so many!" her mom laughed with delight.

"Okay, good," she said, then told Maeve that she'd make her a doctor's appointment for birth control.

"Anything you tell the doctor will be confidential," she said. "You can ask me anything, or tell me anything, sweetheart, but I want you to have someone else to talk to." Her mother's feeling was that Maeve was free to do what she wished, and a mother's only business was to protect her child from harm. So she asked over breakfast if Maeve needed more condoms, then left her to make her own choices. She took good care of her daughter. As far as Maeve knew, her mother never had sex with anyone but her father, closed that part of her life just as Maeve was opening it up.

Maeve's mom went to every soccer game, every swim meet, every dance performance. She brought her orange slices, sandwiches, flowers. Maeve mastered no sport, no art, nothing except for her keening, but all her hobbies honed her competitiveness, her teamwork; they lengthened her body and strengthened her muscles and toughened her up. Her mother sanitized and bandaged skinned knees, made salt baths for the wounds pointe shoes gave Maeve's feet, offered to go to the court where Maeve played pickup with the local boys. But Maeve said she could go by herself; she wasn't afraid. When she came home with black eyes and bruises, her mom asked if she was okay, and Maeve always said with a grin, "Absolutely." Maeve had a huge appetite as a teenager, loved her mom's cooking and the Peruvian joint down the block. She started ordering beers when she was sixteen.

Maeve was always a little ahead of the rest of us.

Maeve took the subway to Manhattan. Several of us saw her there. She didn't mind the stares, girl in a goth dress on the train; everyone knew who she was, and New Yorkers are respectful, so no one asked for an autograph or selfie. They knew what today was.

She'd asked to use the Sky Room at the New Museum, and they said it would be an honor. The *Trigger: Gender as a Weapon and a Tool* exhibit was still on, so guests ascended through videos of Marsha P. Johnson singing; an urn that was also a woman bending over; sculptures Vaginal Davis made out of Aqua Net and cheap red nail polish; neon signs about reclaiming your body through sex after violence; documentaries about women-only institutions; Audre Lorde reminding us of the power of the erotic. Art was the only thing that helped.

And then they emerged on the top floor into a room filled with light. The walls were entirely windows so sunshine streamed onto everyone's skin, the Bowery laid out before them, water towers and tenements and bridges both grimy and gleaming. Crowds of the uninvited gathered in the streets and fire escapes, hoping to hear the wails of the orphaned keener. Many of us were out there, watching.

Maeve ascended in the lime elevator filled with white noise, staring at herself in the mirrored doors. One of us was inside that box with her, with the crowd.

Maeve joined her mother on the balcony, everyone else inside glass.

She hadn't seen her mother for two days, the longest they'd been apart in ages. Even filled with embalming fluid, she was glowing. Her jet hair streaked with silver, her strong shoulders, her pointed chin and sharp nose, Maeve hoped she could remember it all.

Everyone was hushed.

Maeve didn't say a word.

At first, she silently cried, looking straight ahead at the skyline, not down at her mother. Then she collapsed over her mother and sobbed, her body shaking. The only sounds were her weeping; she didn't sing, she didn't scream, she didn't perform. No one needed to hear the lineage, the listing of who remained as a comfort to those left, because only she was left, and she knew the lineage. So did Evelyn; she'd recited it at the wake. Instead, Maeve lamented without language for the first time in her career, for the first time in her life. It went on longer than anyone thought it could. Finally, all the guests left, and Maeve was alone with her mother.

She finally stood, touched her mother's cheek with her fingertips. She took her father's ring off her mother's right thumb and put it on her own middle finger. She took her mother's ring off her left ring finger and put in on her own right. Her parents' rings next to each other, her left hand bare.

Then she turned her back and walked away.

Some of us saw Evelyn crying alongside Maeve, inside the glass with us. She knew she wasn't supposed to. She knew Maeve did it so we didn't have to. But she couldn't keep the tears inside of her. She was inaudible so that most people wouldn't know.   She was watching Maeve change everything.

She looked like she wanted to wail and bawl. She looked like she wanted to sing. Evelyn was thinking of everything ahead of her.

Maeve was only thinking of her mother.

The reviews said it was Maeve's best work. Spare. Minimalist. Surprising. All of Maeve McNamara's art had been leading to this moment—at last a calling into question of the performance of mourning. She had to do something groundbreaking to honor her mother, the one who taught her her trade, trained her, raised her; we knew Maeve had to outdo herself, but we had no idea how she would do it. By showing us her actual grief, not exaggerated, embellished, or amplified, like we'd grown to expect, she startled and stunned us all. Her most powerful performance consisted of not performing at all. And by sweeping aside hundreds of years of tradition so brazenly, she opened up new possibilities and potential for the craft.

All keeners have to contend with Maeve's oeuvre, the agreed-upon master, but now even more so. Can only the greats disregard decorum? Can only the canonized violate convention? Can art only innovate when it's personal?

We didn't know we were still capable of being shocked.

And, of course, some critics called bullshit, said not performing is simply not performing, not a grand expansion of the genre. The most intense criticism was that Maeve dishonored her mother and her profession by refusing to do her duty, by not giving us what we needed: closure. Some said they couldn't heal without the song—that was the whole point. They called her selfish. They called for her to be disbarred.

When the denigrators and the worshippers both said only Maeve McNamara would have dared do such a thing, they were both right.

We thought Maeve's keen for her mother was exquisite. She'd already shown us her virtuosity, already gifted us with her genius. There was no way she could impress us more. Then she lifted her entire vocation to another plane. By just being a human, she became even more heroic. This most recent keen both contained and surpassed everything that had come before. We couldn't wait to see what she'd do next.

And we remember this one because it taught us there are depths of sorrow we have never yet known. Some of us have lost everything.

CHAPTER EIGHT

I don't remember getting home. I sat frozen on the kitchen floor, utterly unsure of what to do next.

My cell phone was in my pocket. That and one credit card, the key to my apartment, and my Metrocard. Vera Wang had known to give my mother pockets on her wedding day. Clare and Vera and I were not the kind of women to carry purses. I called the only person I could think to call, Maxwell Jackson.

"Hey, friend," he said. "I left my phone on in case."

Only then did I realize it was late. I knew sad people were manipulative. "I'm so sorry…"

"Don't be. You know that. I wanted to hug you at the funeral, but that's not how it turned out." Max gave the best hugs. "How are you holding up?"

"Will you write my suicide note?" I asked.

"How serious are you?" Max's voice was calm and kind. I loved how unafraid he was.

"I don't want this to kill me, Max. But I'm afraid it might."

"Okay."

"Everything feels stupid and pointless."

"You know my policy, Maeve. If you decide to hire me, I won't try to talk you out of this. But I will talk to you about this." He paused. "Do you want me to come over?"

"I'm on the floor."

"That's okay. That's an okay place to be. I'm not real strong, but I think I can pick you up. You're too skinny these days, M."

"I'm still in my mourning clothes. I can't manage

to take a bath." Max found his girlfriend in the bath. That's why he started his business. Because her note had no art to it. "Oh, shit, Max, I'm sorry."

"It's fine, Maeve. Really. It's not the same thing. I'd be happy to come over, get you out of your funeral clothes, give you a bath. I'd be happy to see that gorgeous body of yours underwater. You're still alive."

"It feels like barely."

"Barely is fine. Barely is enough for now. We'll get through this. Or we won't. We'll figure it out."

"Thank you, Max. I know it's a lot to ask."

"You'd do it for me."

I would. I told him. He said he knew. "I'll be right over, okay? Don't do anything until I get there."

"I don't think I can do anything."

"Okay. But just in case. Okay? Stay there, Maeve?"

Beautiful Max, whose masculinity was so stunning to me but baffling to him, whose lanky arms and long fingers, the curvatures of his chest, electrified me but I never spoke of his body because it was foreign to him. Max, who wore suits and blouses, panties and Oxfords, tight velour pants and velvet shirts and Carhartts, who wore beaded bracelets and black t-shirts, I saw him, but I always tried to tell him what I saw in the language he needed to hear it in. I told him he was pretty. His body troubled him the way my mind troubled me. He didn't tell me much about my body, he knew I didn't care much about my body, but the way he touched it told me how he saw me. He never performed. He had no public persona. His work was anonymous: you had to read his classified ad right to get to him. But in whatever space he was in, he just shone.

I didn't have language for any of this when I saw

him; I couldn't climb out of my own misery enough
to really connect with anyone anywhere, but when I
remember this night, I remember that all my good
thoughts of him ever were there in his essence when he
walked through my door.

I was still on the floor. "Can I hold you?" he asked.
He always asked, until we got to that point where my
body was my language. I incrementally nodded, and he
wrapped himself around me on the ground, impossibly
awkward. I'm sure it was uncomfortable for him, and
yet so soothing. After as many breaths as it was, he said,
"I'm going to lift you up, okay?" I nodded. Then we were
sitting on the floor. He poured us two glasses of Buffalo
Trace, the best table whiskey around, and I realized it
was my first drink of the day. Too sad even to get trashed.
He didn't make me talk. I said, "Tell me about you." And
he told me about his latest work, a sick man who didn't
want to travel for euthanasia; a mother who decided she
couldn't do that to her kid, not right now, and vowed to
stay another year; a teenager, the hardest ones for him,
but sometimes some people just know it is not going to
get better for them. I asked what else. He said he tried
the Afghani place in deep Brooklyn finally, and it was
as good as I had said. I put my hand on the skin under
his trousers, smooth. I was the first person to shave his
legs, years ago, when I said if he didn't like his body hair,
he didn't have to have it. He asked who took care of me
before, and I said Nymph and he smiled. "Yes, she did
this to my hair," I said. "I love it," he said. "It's so you."
I still hadn't really looked at it. "Alright," he said. "Let's
go be alive in a bathtub, okay?" He pulled me up by my
hands, and when it was clear I didn't need to lean on
him, he guided me to the bathroom, gentle as he always
was in all things, except when gentleness wasn't called
for, and he sat me on the closed toilet while he ran the

bath because where else is there to sit in a bathroom? When he couldn't find anything to put in it, he went to the kitchen and got my grapefruit dishwashing liquid. I almost smiled. I said, "Why is cleansing what I need right now?" thinking of muscular Nymph with her broad shoulders massaging my head, and he said, "You need any kind of care right now. You can feel this." And I could. I felt heat. He undid my wedding dress, and that made both of us actually smile, a betrothal. He held my hands as I stepped in, and when I sank, I felt like there was nothing required of me at the moment. He asked if he should stay or go, and I said stay; Talk or don't? and I said don't, please. Music? No, thank you. I just lay there, doing nothing, until the water cooled, and he asked if he should warm it. No. Can I take you to your bedroom? Yes. He left, then came back, and when he led me in, I saw that he'd changed my sheets but put a clean blanket on the floor, didn't even dry me off, fucked me there intensely, didn't ease me into it, I didn't need that, fucked me with his hands in my wet short hair squeezing so water dripped down my face, and it wasn't tears. He's really good, when he's with the right person; he can forget his body, or, rather, he comes into it newly and freely. He waited and delayed and paused and quickened so that as soon as I came I could hear him behind me, coming too, his loud, deep voice. That's not always the goal of sex, but it is so nice when that happens. He pulled down the blankets, laid me in my clean bed, tied the condom in a knot and threw it on the floor and then went down on me until I came again, such an additional generosity. He asked if should sleep on the couch, give me space, and I asked him again to stay. I don't mind people who want their space while they sleep, but Max is the kind of guy who I knew would curve behind me all night, keep a hand on my belly, and

70

while I didn't wake in the night, I knew that I wasn't alone.

I don't know how long I slept, but when I woke he was still there but up, wearing my silk flowered robe, and it was so delightful. He'd made coffee but hadn't left for food, my watcher, my protector, not going to leave me alone yet, and he was sitting on my couch, just like the man he was and wasn't.

"Can I lay my head in your lap?" I asked and he invited me in. I was still naked but entirely unsexual. "God, I don't want to need this much help, Max," I said.

"It's okay to need help. People want to help. These are the kinds of things we can't do alone."

"But."

"Look, Maeve, I haven't ever sacrificed for you. And you haven't asked me to. I give what I have to offer."

"I love you, Max."

"And I love you, Maeve. You love a lot of people. It's hard sometimes."

"I just want to be normal, Max. I just want to go to the grocery store and not have anyone take my picture."

"You're past that point, love."

"I just want to, like, go to an office. Have a job that's not my identity."

"You could do that. But you'd quit in a month."

And I laughed. I laughed. He knew me so truly.

"I would like you to eat. At this point, anything is better than nothing. What will you be able to stomach? Burrito from Taco Bell? Steak from Keens? Sushi? Egg cream?"

I thought on that. "Pastrami on rye from Katz's."

"Alright. I'd ask you to come with me, but I don't think you want to be seen right now, right?"

"I only want to be seen by you right now, Max."

"Okay, love. Give me an hour. Can I leave for an

hour?"

I gave him a very confident yes, so he would go; it would make him feel better to feed me, and I felt about half-confident I'd be okay for an hour. I lay on the couch in the sun for that whole hour, and it didn't feel funny or sad that I felt like a cat; it didn't feel like anything.

Max never told anyone about this day. I'd told Nymph ages ago that she could talk to the press: I didn't care about our relationship being public. She was awesome, and I was proud to be her lover and friend. But Max was all mine. Because he never had and never would ask me to belong to him. He didn't do monogamy after Celeste, and I didn't after Jake. Still, he was my steady. We'd been captured by the paparazzi at lunch, bullied at the movies. The papers wondered about seeing us walking around his neighborhood, but we kept our touches behind closed doors. Max was not the type for award shows, so because I never displayed him, no one worried about him too much. We worried about each other. We tried not to make that worry a burden.

When he opened the door and locked it behind him, I got right up and walked to my tiny, two-person table. He poured me a beer, and bubbles on an empty stomach felt so good. Then I ate most of my sandwich sitting there still naked, and it was fucking delicious. Max had gotten the same, the kind of guy who would order the same thing in solidarity. We cooed over our food. We'd both been assholes and broken some hearts in our time, but at this point Max was a really good guy. I wasn't sure what I was.

"I can move my appointments today. What do you need? Want?"

"Um. I think just to rest and be alone? Evelyn is coming over tomorrow, so I'll be checked on soon."

"That's fine. Can you agree to give it another

month?" Max liked setting deadlines.

"A month. Yes."

"And in the meantime?"

"If it gets really bad, I'll call. I really want to live through this, Max."

"You don't need my opinion, Maeve, but I think you will. You've been through everything there is, and most of the time you still like being alive."

"I do," I said, and the smile was for me, not for him.

When he left, I realized I hadn't fucked him the way he most liked. Next time.

Fulaing. Áthas. Dorcadas.
Solas. Scrios. Buile. Nua.
Fulaing. Áthas. Dorcadas.
Solas. Scrios. Buile. Nua.
Fulaing. Áthas. Dorcadas.
Solas. Scrios. Buile. Nua.

CHAPTER NINE

Solas. Scrios. Buile. Nua.
Fulaing. Áthas. Dorcadas.
Solas. Scrios. Buile. Nua.
Fulaing. Áthas. Dorcadas.
Solas. Scrios. Buile. Nua.
Fulaing. Áthas. Dorcadas.
Solas. Scrios. Buile. Nua.

The New Yorker gave her a week, then asked Maeve for a profile. And she told us how Evelyn saved her.

Maeve made coffee. She was still in her pajamas—sweatshirt and pants engulfing her, things Jake had packed along with her clothes when he moved her out of their place, things she had occasionally borrowed from him and was grateful for in times of sorrow. The way they swallowed her up was a cousin to comfort. For the first time, Evelyn wasn't in black. She dressed almost like this was a job interview, charcoal slacks and saffron heels, emerald silk shirt tied at the throat. She looked alert. Maeve made them coffee anyway.

Evelyn was either saying, "How are you?" or "What can I do?" as she reached for the cream in a small pot—Maeve had put out pretty cups and proper serving accoutrements, still a good hostess, out of habit more than ethics—and knocked it over. As white spread across the coffee table, Evelyn looked horrified, tried to catch cream in her hands then scurried to the kitchen for a towel to sop it up. Maeve couldn't make herself feel embarrassed on Evelyn's behalf or amused at her distress. "It's fine," she said to Evelyn's hunched back. "It was wanted where it went."

Evelyn stopped mopping, cream dripping from her one towel. She went back for another, returned, finished restoring order, said, "What?"

Maeve refilled the pitcher, gave Evelyn some cream, asked if she took sugar, then said, "I forget which customs are everyone's now, and which are still just Irish." She made herself a mug with cream and sugar, told herself those calories counted as food, said, "When the faeries need milk, sometimes they spill ours. If we begrudgingly let them have it, they'll be annoyed, and play tricks on us, make the next milk go sour so we can't enjoy it either, hide our keys. So it's best to graciously let them have what they need and just say, 'It was wanted where it went.' I don't have it anymore, but those who have it are no longer in want."

Evelyn smiled. "That's really lovely. I would love to go where I was wanted. To be taken there."

Maeve could see her puzzling over something, and said, "Just ask."

"I know it's too soon. But…"

"Yes, I'm quitting."

"I can't do this without you."

"Sure, you can."

Evelyn took a big breath and said, "I think I have an idea. A way forward for you. And me. Do you want to hear it?" She paused. "We might need whiskey for this."

Maeve admired that Evelyn didn't assume she wanted to talk about this. And she was pleasantly surprised at the diagnosis that she was well enough for mid-afternoon happy hour—but, of course, Evelyn hadn't seen how bad yesterday was. Maeve would never tell her. "There's some bourbon in the cabinet."

"I brought Irish. That okay?"

"Absolutely." Evelyn poured them each three fingers of Powers pulled from her purse, and Maeve was charmed.

Maeve sipped, remembered how much sweeter Irish was than bourbon, and said, "Okay. I'm listening."

"You're an artist," Evelyn began.

"I was an artist. I quit." Maeve wasn't being petulant, just clarifying.

"Okay. But I wonder if you could still be an artist, just a different kind." She paused.

Maeve was perplexed. But interested. "'Kay."

"I think the burden of real people... I understand why you just can't anymore. But what about fiction?"

Maeve had no idea what she was talking about. "'Kay?" she said.

"When you did your Ph.D. in Irish studies, you studied John Millington Synge, yeah?"

"Of course."

"What if we revived *Riders to the Sea*?"

At first, Maeve was too tired to think on it. Evelyn was patient. Maeve drank her whiskey, went back into memory, felt a spark of interest. Back when she studied history to hone her craft. She loved being a student. No one ever remembered to call her Dr. McNamara. "Tell me more," she said. She sounded like herself, for a flash.

"So the final scene—the sisters and mother learn the last son is drowned. We could keen on stage... a way of you teaching me without having to attend another funeral."

"You want me to become an actor?"

"I do. If you want to. It would be a transition for me, get me ready for the real thing. And maybe a way for you to let go of who you were. Of what you did. And think about what next." Evelyn voice just lilted with excitement.

"I would play the mother, and you would play Nora? Or Cathleen?"

When Evelyn said yes, either one, she had such love in her eyes that Maeve's breath hitched. "If you wanted," she added.

"Where?" Maeve asked, and Evelyn's face broke into her big, gorgeous smile.

"I was thinking BAM. They've done such a good job with Beckett."

"Oh, yes," Maeve said. "Did you see Torturro and

Casella in *End Game*?"

"They were magnificent!" Evelyn gushed.

Then they nearly said together, "And Fiona Shaw in *Happy Days*!"

"Oh my god, when they played 'Happy Days' at intermission, from that ridiculous TV show, I laughed so hard."

"I thought I was going to pee my pants!" Then, her voice full of awe, "We were there maybe at the same time!"

"Maybe," Maeve said, smiling.

"The acoustics at BAM are so good," Evelyn said wistfully.

Maeve's voice shifted. "It's an intriguing idea, Evelyn. But I would have to care about something again."

"Well…" Evelyn started. Then she cracked a small grin, which said everything, so that she didn't have to add, *Exactly, Maeve. That's entirely the fucking point*. Maeve could tell she was delighted with herself, that maybe she'd found the exact right thing.

And Maeve couldn't help herself, said, "Those fine white boards, bought in case they found the body of the one son, are just so fucking sad." There was a tinge of joy in her voice.

"Oh, and the dropped stitches in the sock, so they know it's Michael's when his body is found." Evelyn had reverie in her voice. "It's so sad and so perfect." Then her hand flew to her face. "Oh my god. Your father. I didn't. Maeve, I'm so sorry."

"It's okay. You are sweet and thoughtful, Evelyn. But I know I'm not the only person whose loved one was identified by clothing. It's a grand Irish tradition. It's one of the reasons I loved that play in grad school. It made me feel less alone."

Evelyn dropped her hand. "Okay," she said. "I still feel bad, springing that on you."

Maeve shrugged. "It's beautiful, that Synge could imagine what that feels like, without ever having it happen to him." Then, "Sometimes art is the only thing that helps."

"Right," Evelyn said, her smile back. Again, *Maeve, that's entirely the fucking point.*

When we read the story, before we knew the end, we all paused here and held our breath. *Please try, Maeve. Please try*, we all chorused in our heads.

Maeve didn't answer her for a month. Then, she said yes.

When Maeve said to Evelyn, "Let's find out. It's about time I heard what your lungs can do," Evelyn covered her face with her hands, and Maeve pulled them down, told her, "You're allowed to be happy." Evelyn threw her arms around Maeve's neck in elation, and Maeve's next thought was, *Let's find out, let's find out.*

Fulaing. Áthas. Dorcadas.
Solas. Scrios. Buile. Nua.
Fulaing. Áthas. Dorcadas.
Solas. Scrios. Buile. Nua.
Fulaing. Áthas. Dorcadas.
Solas. Scrios. Buile. Nua.

CHAPTER TEN

Solas. Scrios. Buile. Nua.
Fulaing. Áthas. Dorcadas.
Solas. Scrios. Buile. Nua.
Fulaing. Áthas. Dorcadas.
Solas. Scrios. Buile. Nua.
Fulaing. Áthas. Dorcadas.
Solas. Scrios. Buile. Nua.

Their stage was as sparse as possible, matte black spinning wheel, table, ladder to the turf loft, rope hanging from a hook, fine white boards gleaming against the wall. The play opened with Evelyn making bread, lifting it high into the light like a sacrament, slamming it onto the table to knead it, slowly, deliberately cutting two lines into the loaf to let the faeries out—all was not right in this household. She saved the extra flour, scraped it from the table onto a plate.

Then she checked the clothes of the man who washed ashore in Donegal. It would take seven days to walk there, this place no one she knew had ever been. The shirt was of the same stuff as her brother's, but weren't there rolls of it in the shops of Galway? But the sock. It's the second of the third pair she knitted; she'd dropped three stitches, and the number was in there. It was Michael's surely.

Then Maeve entered, the townspeople behind her carrying the other son, Bartley, in a dripping red sail. Head dashed on the rocks, drowned. Both sons gone. After already losing her other sons, Shawn, Sheamus, Stephen, Patch, and her husband, to the sea.

They had the boards for a coffin, but she hadn't thought of the nails. Someone would provide the nails.

When Evelyn and Maeve—as Maurya and as Cathleen—keened together, they sounded like a storm, like a great roaring in the west, worsened when the tide was turned to the wind; like the surf in the east and the surf in the west making a great stir with the two noises when they hit one on the other. When Maeve said, "I am not destitute, for I have one child remaining," at that Evelyn wept anew, to be told that a daughter is as good as a son.

Three nights at BAM. Sold out every night, standing ovations each time.

When Maeve sang, "They're all gone now, and there isn't anything more the sea can do to me," we knew how true that was. When she touched the sock her daughter had stitched, the cloth that made her know her son was dead, we knew Maeve must be thinking of her father. But her voice didn't break when she keened Michael and Bartley because no one new was really dead—it was Maeve saying those things, but it was also Maurya. When we learned that Michael had a clean burial in the far north and Bartley would get a deep grave surely—someone would provide the nails—we felt a deep peace. When Maurya said in Maeve's voice, "No man at all can live forever, and we must be satisfied," we heard a new emotion emerge from her throat. We couldn't wait to see what she'd do next.

The papers unanimously called the play a coup. Everyone was smitten with their vision, Evelyn resplendent and Maeve magnificent. There were calls for them to do *Waiting for Godot* as a musical, to revive Lady Gregory's *Cathleen ni Houlihan* with Lady Gaga as the third, to do a Marina Carr retrospective.

And then they parted ways.

Evelyn became splendid, majestic, we will admit. It didn't take long before when Evelyn approached the coffin, we didn't think of Maeve at all.

And watching Maeve's acting career became the new gift she gave us.

We got to see Maeve experience joy. It brought us such pleasure. We got to watch her admit fear and overcome it. And it made us braver, more willing to learn a new language or run our first marathon or ask that woman out on a date, more willing to learn to hunt or to try that restaurant in the run-down part of town—seeing Maeve experience the range of human emotion beyond grief made us feel like we finally had all of Maeve, made us realize how much we'd been missing, made us want to live the lives we'd always wanted.

We saw that Evelyn and Maeve could give us more separately than they could together, and we saw how right they were.

CHAPTER ELEVEN

Maeve won her first Oscar for her film adaptation of Marina Carr's *Ullaloo*.

Maeve wore the yellow Alexander McQueen dress he'd left her in his will, the most gorgeous thing she owned, for which she'd never yet had a proper occasion. We were all a little shocked to see her not in black. When she paused on the red carpet to smile for the cameras, we heard people whispering, "That dress is from that show where a string quartet played Nirvana." "My God! That's the dress from right when they shifted from 'Rape Me' to 'Smells Like Teen Spirit.'" "Holy shit. I always wondered what happened to that one." "That shift to The Smiths 'This Charming Man' at the end was hilarious. God, he was so funny. That show…" Maeve could hear people humming Nirvana, lightly singing, "I would go out tonight, but I haven't got a stitch to wear," and she actually laughed. It was a gorgeous dress, actually pretty, but asymmetrical enough to be a bit terrifying in McQueen's way; its gigantic tilted skirt with that tulle overlay was unnerving, and the gold filigree headdress and earrings made Maeve look ethereal. Hungry borrowed McQueen's antlers-and-lace headdress, wore a very simple yellow pantsuit underneath. Maeve thought they looked awfully dapper together.

Evelyn watched the show from home and was so proud.

Evelyn's first keen was for Barack Obama, assassinated. The thing we'd all hoped against.

Evelyn wore a black satin pantsuit, off the rack,

her hair natural. She shook Bill Clinton's hand, but hugged Hillary. She daintily ate ribs shipped in from 12 Bones in Asheville, drank two White House Honey Ales, told Michelle and Sasha and Malia how sorry she was. Michelle's hair had turned white overnight. President Ocasio-Cortez looked desolate. Bernie looked afraid. People were trying to laugh and sing, but kept falling into silence, just staring at their hero flat on a table.

They followed the hearse to Lincoln Cemetery, a long parade.

Evelyn stood when it was her turn.

"You changed the world. And the monsters tried to change it back. But they failed. They did damage, but we're stronger than they are. You painted the White House Black and told people like me we could have power, do good, stand at the front of the room. Yes, you were a war criminal, my beloved President. You were also elegant, loving, kind. You let kids touch your hair; you loved that strong woman, your wife; you let your daughters be themselves. You're good at basketball! Oh, why have you left us alone?"

Here Evelyn paused. We all were holding our breath.

"We know why you left us. You never would have chosen to go—you were taken. By those who fear us. I do not forgive them. I have been afraid. I am sure you were often afraid. But you lifted people up in the face of your fear—you did not strike people down. So many kids wanted to be you. And still do. And the man who did this? Some white boys filled with rage want to be him, too. But there are more of us than them. There are more of us than them. There are more of us than them."

Her voice cracked. Tears streamed down her face.

"We will raise strong daughters. We will raise strong sons. We will raise children beyond gender. You made Love Is Love law, and we will teach our children and our families and our friends to love beyond the boundaries we were once shown. Our babies will love all the babies. We watched your hair turn silver as you fought for us for eight long years, and we will not let our grief stop us. We will miss you. We will miss you. You did not die in vain, because anger is stronger than fear."

We thought that was the mic-drop moment, where Evelyn would walk off stage. Instead, she stood there fierce-faced, and a gospel choir entered the space. They sang a medley of spirituals and pop songs, Evelyn's voice rising up and around and through them. We got giddy, and then we remembered something terrible happened, and then we sang along again. We sang along. We'd never done that before. But when a congregation is clapping and shouting like they are at a football game, like they are at church, and when you know all the words, you kind of have to raise up your voice.

"I once was lost but now I'm found, was blind but now I see. Paint the White House Black. Fight the power, you got to fight the powers that be. Anger is a gift." Aretha Franklin was just one of the chorus.

"Just try to do your very best
Stand up be counted with all the rest
For everybody knows about Mississippi goddam
I made you thought I was kiddin'
Picket lines
School boycotts
They try to say it's a communist plot
All I want is equality
For my sister my brother my people and me."

We all missed Nina.

The choir lowered their hands, and Evelyn's voice and body stepped into the silence. "Barack Hussein Obama the second, son of Barack Obama Senior and Stanley Ann Dunham, grandson of Stanley Armour and Madelyn Lee Payne Dunham, and Hussein Onyango and Habiba Akumu Obama, husband of Michelle LaVaughn Robinson Obama, father of Natasha and Malia Ann, leader of this nation, murdered in the street. I will visit your hungry asphalt. I will be prepared to say your name."

This one demonstrated pomp and circumstance that had meaning, an American way to honor a dignitary.

As they exited the graveyard into the blast of paparazzi bulbs, the tear tracks on Evelyn's face lit up like strips of aluminum.

Maeve said, "You'll keen me of course."

Shocked, Evelyn said, "But you'll never die."

Maeve didn't respond, just smiled and cocked her head as if to say, *Try again*.

Evelyn took a visible breath, then said, "Yes. Of course, I will."

PART TWO
CHAPTER TWELVE

We keened MC Release on the abandoned Nevins Street platform.

For her, we needed an underground party. Those of us raised up in the counterculture knew the spots to use: the abandoned manufacturing plants where we'd had raves, the foreclosed homes where we'd squatted, the gymnasiums in the now-defunded schools where we'd seen Fugazi play, the gazebos at the fairground where punk bands used to plug in and scream into the woods, all those spaces we'd made ours in our youth, we made ours again in our sorrow.

The tech geeks and cyber nerds made untraceable communication. There was a password to enter. Part party, part protest, the potluck after let people eat food from nations they'd never visited.

All an offshoot of how Evelyn made keens participatory, made more space for deviation from tradition. Evelyn made mourning a little more porous, a little more collaborative. It started with someone crying silently, but visibly. No one responded to that small violation of taboo. It happened sometimes. Then Evelyn saw someone wipe tears off someone else's face. That acknowledgement gave others permission. So at the next keen, when Evelyn asked, "Where have you gone?"—because she was good at her job—her posture and gesture and face told the audience that they were actually invited to respond.

Someone said, "Away." Someone else said, "Home." A third said, "Both."

That was all for that day, but because information travels even without explicit conveyance, at the next ceremony, people were ready to answer Evelyn's call.

Then it continued to evolve in the way of all art: fuck around and find out. Soon people told Evelyn why their beloved had left. Soon they helped her list the lineage. Soon people were dancing, singing, improvising their own additions to the litany.

It was the best jazz ever.

We'd understood grief to be so debilitating we could only let one person feel it. Or—show it. But then… then there was just so much grief. We couldn't pretend to not feel it anymore, we couldn't stop ourselves from showing what we felt.

Evelyn saw this, so instead of being a conduit for our grief, she channeled us into a chorus. We performed the catharsis with her instead of just watching it.

And then Evelyn brought pleasure into mourning. She figured out what Maeve knew but couldn't act on—there needs to be joy in all of it. Maeve hadn't yet really survived, but Evelyn had. She could see beauty from the other side of suffering. Evelyn knew that loving and losing were worth it. The pain of being gone meant they had been here. So, to say goodbye, we needed to party a li'l bit. That, the most apt articulation of loss.

A merry wake paired with a collective keen could start a riot.

Evelyn brought new fans to the form. People who'd thought keening was staid, passé, bad, felt new life brought to it through her. They joined us.

So here we were, the b girls making MC Release's body twerk while the techno kids, now grown, traced chemiluminescent arcs through the dim air of the 2345 lower-level station, unused. Evelyn watched the grace of the hands holding lit wands, chartreuse and fuchsia, lilac and turquoise. She let the rhythm lull and steady her. She watched the b boys and b girls spinning and posing on cardboard and let them enliven her. She remembered watching music videos alone in her room when she was a kid, hip-hop and metal and punk, remembered how much she wanted to be beautiful and fierce. How much she wanted to perform. Shine.

Gaia was graffitiing a wall to the same rhythm of everyone's dance, her stylized words more image than language, but some could read *CALAMITY*, *ABANDON*, *RESILIENCE*, *KEEN*. *SORROW SORROW GRIEF MOURNING GONE GONE GONE*. *ALIVE*.

Swagger first.

Evelyn stepped up, and Yasiin Bey and Queen Bey stepped to her sides. She said no words of her own, just quoted MC Release, the finest sampler of the decade. She mashed up MC Release's mashups, quoting metal bands singing about hope, hip-hop artists singing about home, everyone somehow singing about love.

Thom Yorke and Bjork grinned when they heard their words in her voice. Yasiin threw his hand in the air. Zach threw his fist in the air. Killer Mike openly cried at the turntables. We all missed MJK.

We pieced it together like we would set lists after shows. The beat from *the* Ms. Jackson with "Miss Jackson" over it! Oh my god the way *everyone* started dancing when "Rhythm Nation" came on with Outkast's chorus. Turns out, we all still know all the words.

She quoted Erykah Badu being herself on an album named after a line from a W.B. Yeats poem; oh, no, probably that album was quoting the novel by Chinua Achebe, quoting Yeats, right?

The sick beat was from "Idioteque," yeah? Yeah, but she ran Tool over it. Then that beat from "Reckoner" but with Rage lyrics. And "Brooklyn" in the background while she did "Priority" over it, with Bey and Bey? *The Ecstatic* was named after that Victor LaValle novel. Oh yeah, I forgot that.

Sanctioned bootleg cassette tapes were available immediately after. Evelyn didn't say a word of her own. It was magic.

The party carried on. The food was abundant. No way to keep things hot, so everyone ate seaweed salad and deviled eggs and sesame noodles and California rolls and chips and salsa and dolmas and tabouli. And plenty of booze.

Evelyn wandered. A bit more comfortable around celebrity now, though she didn't yet understand that she herself was famous, she tried to speak to as many people as she could at every keen.

Of course, Banksy was there. When she handed Evelyn a card and said, "I want you to keen me when I'm gone, and this is me trusting you not to out me before that," Evelyn threw her a look like, *Girl, please*.

"Hey, I had to say it."

"No, you did not. If you're asking me, you must respect me, so please respect how much I fucking respect you."

"Alright. Heard," Banksy said, but did not apologize.

Which made Evelyn fall a little bit more in love. So she said, "Good," instead of, "Thank you."

Then she said, "My favorite is the Extinction Rebellion one. That mantra has gotten me through a lot of days." *From this moment despair ends and tactics begin*.

"Thank you. I'd have guessed the anarchy one

would be your favorite." *A mom adjusts her punk son's mask for a protest, tells him, You be careful out there, and follow Black leadership. Anarchy does not mean chaos, it means community care and support. And he responds, Yes, mama.*

"Oh please," Evelyn responded. "Too obvious."

They both laughed, and hugged, and that felt really good.

That Banksy was Black and British was something we all sort of expected, but that she was a she, only Evelyn felt certain of before she knew for sure. She loved when her intuition was right.

We know this because we were there.

Listening to Evelyn and Banksy chat, remembering the masks, the protests, we thought, *We got through that time when so many of us died.*

We know that who counts as "us" is different for each person.

We weren't deep enough underground that our phones didn't work, and when she stepped away from Banksy, Evelyn got an alert that Klee Benally passed. She told us that she knew she lived on occupied Lenape territory because of him. Evelyn wanted to keen him, wanted mourners to light his pyre with Molotov cocktails, but she assumed that wasn't the Diné tradition. His community didn't need to hire her. So she made a donation in his name to Kinłani Mutual Aid, then went and made a plate with the last of the revelers.

This keen reminded to us that we are a community that is alive and vibrant, even as we lose members daily. Some join us. We are still here.

When *Teen Vogue* asked to interview Evelyn, they asked her about her past, and she declined to respond, saying instead, "I would like to keep that private. Thank you for understanding."

When asked about her present, she shook her head. "Some people want to be wholly known. I want your readers to know they can choose what parts of themselves they give away."

They were outraged, of course, because they were entranced. They wanted all of her, all of her. To know if they could be her, become her.

But some of us understood. Who she had been didn't matter; just who she was, and what she did.

CHAPTER THIRTEEN

On their walk to a daytime keen, a Tuesday, when Maeve doesn't have a matinée and can walk with Evelyn, Maeve says, "I love that picture of you and Quinn in *The New York Post.*"

"Ha! Thanks. Pregnant in a tuxedo—the paparazzi didn't know what to do. But didn't they look fetching?" Evelyn's partner went with her to the opening of *Sonny's Blues* wearing a black tux, blue velvet heels, blue lips and mascara, and a shellacked comb-back. With a round, massive belly. Evelyn wore sapphire, cerulean, cobalt. All the deepest blues.

"You're a gorgeous couple."

"Thank you. The photographer asked me, 'Who's the father?' I answered, 'Does it matter?'"

"Jesus."

"Then, 'Boy or girl?' And I answered, 'Does it matter?'"

"You're great. Did you pick a name?"

"Oh! Yes. Azure."

"Of course. I love it."

"I hope the kid will love it. And can keep it, whatever gender they are." Evelyn is very, very in love with her person. "And…" she adds, "you were stunning in *The Day the Bird Flu Came*. Just… riveting. I couldn't take my eyes off of you."

"Wow. Thanks."

"You must know how good you were."

Maeve shrugs. "The role felt good. It felt right."

"You're on the path, Maeve. I know it's drudgery sometimes. But… I'm grateful for you."

"I don't know what I would do without you," Maeve says, then pulls Evelyn into a bone-pressing hug.

They walk quickly in their clicking heels, stepping over subway grates on the balls of their feet like all femme New Yorkers know how to do.

Rosa Macias was a mother who had been released from ICE custody without her sons. She drowned herself in the river. She and her sons were trying to get to some relatives' apartment when they were detained. As far as we know, the children are still being held.

Someone is coughing because a prankster got some pepper into the tobacco. An old man is trying to stand, but his coat is stitched to his chair. A kid trips because someone tied his shoelaces together. The corpse on the kitchen table shakes, and Evelyn screams a little and hears laughter under the tablecloth.

Everyone turns to look, and she and Maeve wave.

The family goes right back to the merrymaking, but it's a bit more strained, now that everyone knows the tone is about to shift.

The cousins try to lift the corpse, feats of strength.

The husband who had FaceTimed Evelyn to set up the ceremony is eliciting confession from an abuela who is saying the most outrageous things. He gives her a shot of mezcal as penance.

"To keep her from becoming La Llorona," the husband had said when he'd called. "We believe we'll get the boys. But their mother must have feared their death, felt she couldn't save them, felt it was her fault, and we don't want her grief keeping her stuck in this world." So this keen is more casting a spell of release for the dead than for the living. So okay. Evelyn believes enough in witchery.

Candles are everywhere, Jesus and Mary and saints whose names she doesn't know and creatures painted on glass that look more pagan than saintly. Green and red and blue and yellow flames, little lit gems on every surface. The kitchen has yellow walls and lace curtains.

Everyone quiets. Maeve steps back, and Evelyn begins. "Why are we now alone? Did we not love you enough for you to stay?" She knows love isn't enough to keep anyone here, but she wishes it were. "Why is your beauty now gone?" Evelyn tries to take the sadness out of the bodies and put it in the air.

"We curse the river that took you. We damn the water that filled your lungs. May it boil away to oblivion. May the current of your destruction suffer as we suffer."

Evelyn shifts to just sounds, the range of all the ways women of her kind are said to sound in Ireland. A proper Irish keen to prevent a Mexican folk story from becoming true. This custom exists all over the world; we just know the most about the Irish version because they have the most written history. In Leinster in the east, her wails are said to be so piercing they can shatter glass. In Kerry in the west, her cries are said to be a low, pleasant singing. In Tyrone in the north, her keens are the sound of two boards being struck together. In the farthest north, Rathlin Island, she is said to sound like barn owls. She sounds like everyone that has come before her. Evelyn screams, screeches, and shrieks, and no one covers their ears.

"You did what you had to do, but we wish there was another way. Fuck the government that took you from us. May this nation become what it says it is."

Everyone starts wailing without words, and Evelyn is done.

Evelyn performed what we already intuited but hadn't yet seen: all grief is worth honoring, even that which is not televised.

Evelyn just cannot bring any fucking joy into this one.

The father they were trying to get to hands Evelyn and Maeve each a mezcal. They throw it back without lime or salt, as is the custom. He cocks his head and asks, "Another?"

"Yes, please."

Maeve throws it back and gets a third while Evelyn sips the smokiness, and they make plates: stews seasoned deep red, rice, beans. "That's spicy," he says while pointing to a salsa that looks like confetti, and Evelyn says that is fine as she scoops some on top of chips. "That's tongue," he says, and she puts some on her plate and says that is fine, too. "I like intensity," she says. With his middle finger he hooks a bottle by the neck and carries it to the couch.

At least pleasure, if not joy.

They eat on the couch with plates balanced on their knees.

"Do you think she's in hell?" he asks.

"Definitely not," Evelyn says. "You are. But she's fine."

He puts his face in his hands and Evelyn puts her palm on his back.

After a minute she says to him, "You will get them back. They will be traumatized. This never should have happened. She couldn't hold it. But you can. And you will." She refills their small glasses with aged agave and he looks up, the planes of his face slicked with tears. He doesn't wipe them away, and neither does Evelyn. They drink and eat, and as she crunches the salt crystals on the thick chips—rolled out, cut, and fried by hand in the tortillaria down the block—in her molars, Evelyn feels like she is consuming Francisco's tears. She bites a pickled jalapeño, and that tang of brine intensifies the heat in her mouth.

"You're not going to hell, now, right?" he asks.

"It used to be taboo to wake a self-killing." He winces. "But I'm not so traditional as some." She smiles. Maeve can't look at anyone. "I mean, I know the tradition well enough to know when it no longer serves us. Maeve does too. Learned it rough. The worst that will happen is I piss off the ancestors. I'm willing to take that risk." Evelyn knows that all of her ancient relatives, even the mineral star dust that made them, are inside of her, and she knows they approve.

At least he smiles. The salsa is hot, he was right about that. The mezcal makes her mouth hotter. This will never be over for him.

"I should work the room," she says, but he gently grasps her wrist.

"Please don't make me talk to anyone else," he asks.

"Okay," she says, and she and Maeve settle in.

Fulaing. Áthas. Dorcadas.
Solas. Scrios. Buile. Nua.
Fulaing. Áthas. Dorcadas.
Solas. Scrios. Buile. Nua.
Fulaing. Áthas. Dorcadas.
Solas. Scrios. Buile. Nua.

CHAPTER FOURTEEN

Solas. Scrios. Buile. Nua.
Fulaing. Áthas. Dorcadas.
Solas. Scrios. Buile. Nua.
Fulaing. Áthas. Dorcadas.
Solas. Scrios. Buile. Nua.
Fulaing. Áthas. Dorcadas.
Solas. Scrios. Buile. Nua.

Sunday Evelyn goes to Coney Island in the snow.
Everything bleached and dirty, the tenements
on fire, steam from hundreds of radiators drifting from
roofs, it is one of those unseasonable weather days in
New York where she looks out the window and the sky is
white so she wears gloves, a hoodie and a jacket, a scarf
and two pairs of socks. She steps outside, expecting the
ammonia stab in the back of her throat, but the air slips
into her lungs easily

She walks past where you can buy clams, beer,
corn on the cob, hotdogs, and cotton candy in the
summer, past where you creak-step down the salt-
saturated boards, grease staining paper containers of
onion rings and mozzarella sticks, cartoon signs of
everything you're eating on the front of the tiny stand
selling it, bad draft beer so cold it's worth the bathroom
you have to pee in.

She walks past the amusement park, the place
so packed with bodies in the summer you can't tell
that everything is peeling, old and unreplaced, where
bulbs from a starlet's dressing-room mirror adorn every
corner, where decades-old rides are lit with every color
of neon, this place made to maintain our idea that joy is
sustainable, only some people are miserable, not anyone
here.

She walks past the Cyclone, the oldest wooden
roller coaster in the world; it bangs you up, rattles, five
bucks a ride, but when it's over, the carnies will let you
give them three for another.

She walks past the Parachute Tower, the tall, red,
Brooklyn-style Eiffel-scaffold, and Evelyn wants to climb
it, see out to the horizon on all sides, look out over a flat

landscape with inflated children's toys rising up out of it, the things that make memorabilia—pale carnival rides without their lights, a pier trailing out into the ocean. She wants to see people with metal detectors scanning the snowy beach, old men fishing, the haunted house, water slide, arcade, batting cage, bumper cars, miniature golf course, flick-a-ring-onto-a-bottle-and-win-a-teddy-bear-or-a-goldfish game, kiddie roller coaster, tilt-a-whirl, pirate ship, all the rides that lie locked up in a lot, behind chainlink fences, in winter.

But she has a job to do.

Hushed and incubated, the whole world, clouds, sky, sun, all different shades of white. The sound of sand crunching under her feet, waves rolling, melting the snow, and she a little too warm in her layers. She can see the sky out here.

They always say they're going to tear it down. Leave some of the relics—the Wonder Wheel, Cyclone, minor league baseball park. None of the businesses down the boardwalk. Instead, luxury condos, "amusements," fancy restaurants, turn it into the Disneyland they've made of Times Square, no more pimps and peepshows.

But this remains the one place gentrification can't touch.

The merry-go-round will run next summer. Children will sit astride its wood-carved creatures, claim a Pegasus, elephant, zebra, rhinoceros, dragon, hippopotamus, giraffe, hippogriff, tiger, or beautiful mare as their own, squeal as the gears speed up and they spin faster. Parents will watch and wave, some will ride for old time's sake; teenagers on dates will climb on trying to be suave in their tight or loose clothing, and they will giddily laugh and dare each other to reach for the golden ring, one of the few remaining carousels

104

in the world still with a golden ring, and they'll grab for it. Every time they pass, they'll stretch for it, hold the bars and reach their arms out as far as they will go; they'll stand on their dolphins or lions, but they still can't touch it. You can't get it: it's impossible; no one has ever gotten it, but everyone wants to try, everyone longs to stretch beyond what they're able, all of us whirling around think about leaping off our fading and peeling stallions or unicorns and grabbing it in the air; everyone wants to try, and some still do.

Today, she doesn't hear calliope.

She walks into the building where the sideshow runs all day, the rows of worn bleachers filling from stage right, emptying from stage left. Once you've seen the same act twice, you've seen the whole show. The building where the sword swallowers, glass eaters, the Fat Lady of the Circus named Helen Melon, and the bed-of-nails walkers work. Ravi, the Bendable Boy from Bombay, claims he was stung by scorpions as a child, and instead of killing him, the poison made his bones flexible. Insectavora's feet were toughened by volcanic rocks when she was a hermit on Fiji; now, she climbs a ladder of swords and swallows fire, her face tattooed and pierced, a stabbed canvas. Heather, the former Mormon who kept her normal name, was struck by lightning as a child and can now endure deadly amounts of electricity zapped through her body which is so sexy she was never going to stay a Mormon, was bound to run away from the Midwest plains and join the circus. Home of the Sideshow School, where they will teach you how to suppress the gag reflex, where every year new students learn to pound nails up their noses.

Maeve is there. All the mermaids are there.

Evelyn takes off her layers to reveal her costume: striped tights under a tutu, the first time she is not all in black.

She begins. "CURIOSITIES. WONDERS. SIDESHOWS.

Self-described freaks.

I am what you are. I am what you are. I am what you are."

But Evelyn isn't a freak to us. This keen makes us realize that all of us can feel like freaks, even those of us who seem to fit in.

"I want to be what you are. Visceral entertainment. Make you applaud or scream or close your eyes or throw up.

This place was built over one hundred years ago and it never burned.

Freaks used to be exploited because they couldn't find work elsewhere. But now you—you are celebrated.

One million people have watched you blow flames, swallow chains, juggle knives, walk on glass, charm snakes. No blood or nudity, just All-American weird.

Every walk of life—rich, poor, middle-class, young, old, every ethnicity, every sexuality, every gender, everybody in between, all sit under the same roof and laugh and are happy. People get scared, storm out. But most just need their hand held as they cross the threshold.

You held our hand as we crossed the threshold.

We are holding your hand now, KooKoo.

You are willing to put your lives on the line seven times a day for an audience of two or fifty or one hundred.

You keep live entertainment alive."

She pauses, while the audience watches the corps do everything she's just described.

"And KooKoo the Bird Girl, she spun and she

flew above nails. We never feared she'd fall, but we knew she could.

This second KooKoo—who looked uncannily like the first KooKoo who performed here decades ago—our KooKoo reincarnated and reclaimed her predecessor, the only person in the world who could bring her back to life.

And now she has left us.

We will miss her sequined leotard, her grin, her eyes that saw more than we could ever see, but that some thought were without sight.

She became the core of this culture, the center, she nurtured and led. She celebrated herself.

Sarah Houbolt. You made us all want to be like you. A superhero from a comic book. Magical powers to enchant and enthrall and excite. Daredevil. Acrobat. College graduate. Gold and silver medal Paralympian swimmer. Advocate for equity. Cirque du Soleil performer. Entertainer. Activist. You explored the aesthetics of access. I wish you could have taught me how to hula hoop.

Bearded ladies, tattooed ladies, fat ladies, small people, strong people, all used to be freaks! Thank you, KooKoo, for helping all of us let our freak flags fly. See each other for who we are. You were a star."

Evelyn keeps this one joyful, as is her style, but there is a surprising amount of sorrow in her voice. And somehow this shows us that, like Maeve, Evelyn had lost everyone, too, once. We just don't know that because she never told us.

Then there is yelling. One entrance, one exit, the building suddenly fills with bodies. Men with Confederate flags and one in a hood, and they're all white, and we know whatever they want isn't good.

Maeve finds me across the crowd, catches my eye

and immediately runs for me. She stands between me and them. "It's the Proud Boys. They cannot get you," she says. "You must go."

Insectavora and Lizardman and Mat Fraser help. They put their bodies between me and the fascist racists; they get caught; they get arrested or worse; they take a beating or worse, and I get away to keen another day.

Fulaing. Áthas. Dorcadas.
Solas. Scrios. Buile. Nua.
Fulaing. Áthas. Dorcadas.
Solas. Scrios. Buile. Nua.
Fulaing. Áthas. Dorcadas.
Solas. Scrios. Buile. Nua.

CHAPTER FIFTEEN

Solas. Scrios. Buile. Nua.
Fulaing. Áthas. Dorcadas.
Solas. Scrios. Buile. Nua.
Fulaing. Áthas. Dorcadas.
Solas. Scrios. Buile. Nua.
Fulaing. Áthas. Dorcadas.
Solas. Scrios. Buile. Nua.

CHAPTER SIXTEEN

We always thought he'd emerge.

We wondered who'd been tending to him, always thought we'd learn.

He'd retreated from public life, and, man, we understood that, as much as we missed him. But we figured he was writing while away from us. We figured he would return with something new for us.

So when we hear he's died, it is a new kind of bereavement. James Baldwin. Gone. Again. This time for good.

When Evelyn gets the call, she sits on the ground.

He's now arrived back home in Harlem—they merry waked him where he died, in Saint-Paul de Vence, but he will be buried at home.

Evelyn puts on her Brooklyn Poets Audre Lorde t-shirt, covers it with her Baldwin University sweatshirt made by Philadelphia Printworks, the crew that imagines colleges are named after Black intellectuals instead of slave owners. Jeans and Prada patent pumps. She walks down her stairs and hails a green yellow taxi.

Someone is making a scotch and milk for everyone who enters, and that is perfect. There is no food.

The intensity of being with someone at their worst, both lifting that and deepening it, is the most intense way of being a human Evelyn knows.

It's what Baldwin's art always did for her.

Her friends who'd put their bodies on the line, their bodies between Evelyn and danger, between art and violence, they aren't here. But they are here.

Evelyn takes the stage and places her scotch and

milk on top of the piano with a trembling hand.

And then she sings.

At first just scat, sounds.

The best jazz always pushes itself to the edge of making sense, almost veers out of control, then swerves back. And yes, we see that as a metaphor for life. The musicians up there are the best, and Evelyn riffs over Swell's drums, under Fish's horns, through Jacob's piano.

It's like we watch her steady herself. And it steadies us.

Then Evelyn lets us know that this kind of jazz is also the Blues. She shifts into words, weaving them into and over and under the sounds.

Then we realize she is quoting him. Giving him back to us.

"'There's no way not to suffer—is there?' 'That doesn't stop any of us from trying.' 'Isn't it better, then, just to—take it?' 'But nobody just takes it, that's what I'm telling you. Everybody tries not to. You're just hung up on the way some people try—it's not your way.' 'I don't want to see you die trying not to suffer.' 'I won't die trying not to suffer. At least, not any faster than anybody else.'

"All I know about music is that not many people ever really hear it. What we mainly hear, or hear corroborated, are personal, private, vanishing evocations. But the man who creates the music is hearing something else, is dealing with the roar rising from the void and imposing order on it as it hits the air. Creole began to tell us what the blues were all about. They were not about anything very new. He and his boys up there were keeping it new, at the risk of ruin, destruction, madness, and death, in order to find new ways to make us listen. For, while the tale of how we suffer, and how we are delighted, and how we may triumph is never new, it always must be heard. There isn't any other tale to tell, it's the only light we've got in all this darkness."

The musicians and then the audience begin echoing her. Emphasizing her. *Suffer. Delight. Darkness. Light. Ruin. Madness. New*.

She quotes his conversation with Audre Lorde, and it isn't serious or academic because she makes it lilting, lyric. "'We have to begin to redefine the terms of what woman is, what man is, how we relate to each other.' 'But that demands redefining the terms of the western world...' 'Jimmy, we don't have an argument.' 'I know we don't.' 'But Audre, Audre...' 'I'm here, I'm here... We do not accept terms that will help us destroy each other... In the same way you know how a woman feels, I know how a man feels, because it comes down to human beings being frustrated and distorted because we can't protect the people we love. So now let's start—' 'All right, okay...' 'Let's start with that and deal.'"

She doesn't list the lineage. We know all who came before, everyone, all who come after, everyone. He is the center. Evelyn tells us again of what he's given, what is lost, what will live on.

This one reminds us that the lineage is long, and it includes the periphery.

And when Evelyn is done, she will lift that glass lit indigo, she will drink it down, and she will carry it away.

ACKNOWLEDGEMENTS

Thank you to all of the books, stories, poems, music, art, film, plays, and conversations that made this book—including you, Cormac McCarthy. (You all can read this as ars poetica, if you'd like.)

Thank you to my most excellent Editor, Kyle McCord; my students who are really my teachers, Jonathan Calloway and Tyler Orion; my Revolution, Minky Malone; and my first reader, Justin Bigos; for helping me solidify my ideas. (You all can read this as an essay, or even an autobiography, if you'd like.)

Thank you to the magazines and presses who published excerpts of this novel: *Tupelo Quarterly*, *Isele*, *H_NGM_N* (RIP), *The Tusculum Review*, *The Kenyon Review*, and Indiana University Press.

Thank you to everyone who has heard me read portions of this novel, and who encouraged me to be as vulnerable as possible. (And to set boundaries.)

Thank you to all of my students, colleagues, and friends, who have expanded my lineage.

For the cover, Marielena Andre used a mourning dress from the Brooklyn Museum Costume Collection (Metropolitan Museum of Art). The inspiration for the design began with the book itself and therefore played off Irish concepts and symbols. For example, the Tree of Life image was created as a vector, drawing connection to the notion of lineage and fame. The font selections were based on the author's choice of Didot for the main text, plus Stonecross for the chapter heading underlays, while Futura was used to match the cover and create a merger of contemporary and ancient. For the chapter breaks, Gaelic was used to capture a quote from the final page of the novel: Fulaing, Áthas. Dorcadas. Solas. Scrios. Buile. Nua. This translates to *Suffer. Delight. Darkness. Light. Ruin. Madness. New*.